# MURDER BY THE SEA

## A VIOLET CARLYLE HISTORICAL MYSTERY

## BETH BYERS

# SUMMARY

**September 1925.**

Vi and Jack have fled for the sea shore. Both to enjoy the sea air and to gather up their friend, Rita Russell who's come home at last. A little sea air, a ramble or two, afternoon naps, lingering mornings over a cup of Turkish coffee and perhaps all will be aright again.

Only one morning adventure ends with a body and yet again, Violet, Jack and their friends find themselves involved in a mysterious death. Will they be able to find the killer before he strikes again?

*For Auburn, Tessa, Bonnie, and Carissa who helped me get this*
*baby done*
*with my hand injury*

# CHAPTER 1

The scent of coffee, especially Turkish coffee, was magical. Dark, strong, bitter—Violet felt it must be the scent of heaven. Perhaps that scent would have been perfected by the scent of a recent rain and lavender in the distance. What else would heaven smell like but those things, perfectly combined?

Of course, at that moment, the scent of Turkish coffee combined with a salty, sea breeze *and* the baby Vi in Violet's arms. Heaven. She was transported beyond the moment to a surreal, impossible, wonderland. Leaning down, she breathed in sweet Violet Junior. It seemed that Kate had located a lavender cream that combined with new baby smell and milk breath. Perhaps that was why Violet's theory about heaven's scent was so reliant on a distant lavender field.

Violet glanced up from the baby, grinning at the idea, and caught her husband, Jack, smiling at her. He was holding baby Agatha as though he'd held dozens of babies. She had to admit that a baby looked good on him. He was one of those incredibly large and broad men. The word mountain came to mind. He had big shoulders that seemed to hold up the world, with a heavy jaw, strong arms, and strong hands that held Agatha so carefully. Jack might not have been traditionally handsome, but he was rugged and all that Violet might have desired. There was, she knew, no one more suited to her.

The house they'd taken near the ocean had a large back patio area with tables that allowed them to breakfast outside while their dogs ran. The ocean breeze that had so enchanted Violet rose swiftly and gusted past the table before slowing to rise and fall in tune with the waves in the distance. The ocean wind darted through her favorite people. It swirled around Violet's sister-in-law, Kate, who was savoring a cup of coffee as though she hadn't had one in ages, and then went past Violet's twin brother, Victor, who was shoveling in his breakfast with near desperate speed. Violet rolled her eyes at him and noted the wind ruffling her friend Denny's hair. He was leaned back in his chair, eyes closed, as he snoozed over his loaded breakfast plate.

If she could have followed the wind, she'd have noticed how it went inside the house where Denny's wife, Lila, was coming down the stairs of the house. Or how it seemed to dart up the train tracks to her friend Hamilton Barnes as he was catching a late-morning train from London to Felixstowe to join them for a long weekend by the sea while they waited for their friend Rita's ship to come in.

If Violet could have traced the wind back to its origin over the sea, she'd have seen that same breeze swirl around Rita as she leaned over the rail of a ship and watched the waves crash against her steamship. Next to Rita was a handsome blonde man with round spectacles and an engaging grin. He was the type of man to steal a girl's heart and imagination, and the breeze would bring them both to Violet in the coming hours.

"I never thought that last heat wave would break," Victor told Violet around a mouthful of food.

Violet lifted her brow at Victor, who grinned after he swallowed. He was far more concerned with eating than he was with appeasing Violet. She suspected it came back to the babies in Violet's and Jack's arms. The twins had been through a good three or four nannies so far and we're currently without one.

Little Agatha wrinkled her nose and screwed up her mouth, and Violet considered amending her thoughts about Victor's whining over the nannies. However, Jack placed his hand on Agatha's back and said something in his deep, low voice. At the sound, Agatha blinked at Jack and then settled back against his chest.

Violet clucked down at little Violet and then reached over to rub Agatha's back as Jack unconsciously rocked her.

"They smell new," Violet told Victor. He just nodded, mouth full, but she could hear how he'd respond—'They are new.'

"We're calling her Vivi," Kate told Violet, still not bothering with food when there was Turkish coffee to be had. "To prevent confusion."

"Oh, I like it. I am surprised you were able to get away from your mother so quickly."

Kate's mother, Mrs. Lancaster, was—without question—unwilling to have Kate very far away. "Victor told me that he'd rather remove his skin that continue to linger around my mother. She was correcting his every move with the girls."

Violet gasped and Victor didn't even blink at the sound. He was crazy if he thought that Mrs. Lancaster wouldn't attempt to torture him over the departure.

"I told her that Vivi and Agatha needed their aunt."

"Did she protest?"

"Strenuously," Victor agreed. "Dear, sweet Grandmother Lancaster said I was a fool and the only thing Vivi needed was a clean nappie and a father who had a lick of sense."

"I'd credit you with a lick of sense." Violet nuzzled her nose against Vivi, breathing her deeply in.

"Of course you would," Victor said after guzzling his coffee. "We're compared too often for me to be entirely without sense and you to be unaffected."

Lila moseyed onto the patio a moment later and took in the babies, Victor frantically eating, and Kate sipping her coffee with dark circles under her eyes. "You need to hire a nanny."

"We have," Kate said, "three times. None of them are good enough for Vivi and Agatha. Victor fires the poor women the first time he finds one of the babies wailing."

Victor just lifted a brow, his gaze moving from each of the twins to Violet.

"Seems reasonable to me," Violet answered.

"I'm tired," Kate muttered. "I didn't sleep the last few months before they were born and I haven't slept since."

"I wonder," Violet offered, "if I might take them for a long walk after they eat? You could have a nap."

"Yes," Kate said without waiting a moment to even breathe. She shoved her coffee aside and said, "Give me Vivi. I'll feed her first."

Kate took the baby and left while Lila watched the young mother go. There was a look of consternation of Lila's face and Victor was staring at Violet in gratitude, though he had to have known when they'd agreed to come that a nap was guaranteed.

"Don't have two at one go, Vi darling," Victor said. "They wake in turns, and Kate and I never get a breath of sleep."

Violet imagined that having twins would be excellent fun once they slept through the night, and she hoped to have help that she trusted. Victor really should have worked at finding someone *before* the babies arrived. She suspected he'd hired the first person he kind of liked, ended up not liking her, and then hired another in a vicious cycle.

"Victor—" Violet didn't need to expand on her thoughts; he knew what she was thinking, and her brother's wince told her that he was cursing himself as well.

Jack changed the subject. "We need to meet Hamilton at the train station. We could have a boy bring his bags back and make him walk with us. I suspect that Hamilton might have some worries to get out."

"Back to the matter at hand," Lila said, looking at Victor. "You need a nanny, and I know one."

"No," Victor said, shaking his head without a moment's wait.

"Trust me," Lila snapped.

"Why aren't you hiring her? You're expecting a little bundle of screaming and vomit."

"I *already* hired her sister. They're both good, but I'm not expecting my *angel* for a while. The one I hired will be available when I need her. The sister *you* should hire is available now."

"No," Victor said. "Just because you met them doesn't mean they're good. I have been down this road three times."

"Exactly," Denny said lazily, eyes still closed. "Lila is thinking ahead and doing her research."

"Lila knows you'll be useless, unlike me," Victor shot back.

Lila ignored both of them and continued, "They're named Poppy and Jane, and they're older, mid-50s perhaps. Both of them with decades of experience and *excellent* references."

"No," Victor said, his gaze fixed on Agatha in Jack's arms.

"They also worked as nurses during the Great War," Lila added. "They have *both* nursing experience and experience with babies and little children."

Victor paused and then shook his head. "Why aren't they nursing then?"

"They only did that to help with the war. Their passion is raising happy babies. They focus on the *happy* too. Lots of time outdoors as they get older, lots of nature walks and fresh air. Ruddy-faced little darlings. Victor—they only considered *us* because they like the idea of working for families who spend so much time together."

His gaze narrowed on her and she placed her hand over her heart. "I swear they've literally raised dozens of babies. Stayed with families for years through the babyhood. Denny visited a number of their former children. They really are excellent."

"Denny?" Victor scoffed.

"He's determined we're having a daughter," Lila told Victor, glancing at Kate. "He says she needs a good foundation and we're incapable of truly providing it. He even hired that private investigator to check these women out."

"The honest one or the shady, but pretty one?" Violet demanded. "Did he hire John Smith?"

"Smith. I am certain that Poppy and Jane's rooms were searched, their journals were read, their former children were interviewed. These women know what they're doing."

Kate returned from feeding Vivi to take Agatha. They all winced at the exhaustion on Kate's face, and Lila added—nearly begging, "I am not strong like Kate. I can't be a wrung out dishrag like your poor wife. I need a good woman to help me. And—" Lila's smile was wicked. "I already hired them. They're both coming on a part-time working vacation to help with the twins. They'll be here and you can test them out. Though, however, I will be hiring Poppy."

"Why do you get that one?"

"The other one's name is Jane, and I just don't like it. I have known too many mean Janes."

"I don't know," Victor muttered, taking the sleeping Vivi from Kate.

"You don't get to decide," Kate told him. "Not when I'm this tired. We're hiring these women, popping in on them between all of us, and I'm going to nap every single day."

"Kate—"

She scowled at him as she hissed in stilted periodic statements. "Every single day. I am going to nap." A light seemed to flow over her face as she added, "Until I wake on my own."

"Kate—"

"They're already hired," Lila reminded him. "You need the help. Accept it."

But it was Violet who made it all better. "We'll all be here, Vic. We'll make sure the babies are safe and happy and that we all like these women. You might as well give it a chance. Kate is tired."

Victor hesitated.

"You're tired too. You aren't thinking clearly. You're imagining the worst, but the worst *will not* happen to the twins. Not with all of us looking after them."

Victor searched Violet's face with his matching gaze. They had the same eyes, the same sharp features, the same witty expressions, but Victor truly was dulled with exhaustion. "Do you promise?"

"I do," she swore, taking baby Vivi.

# CHAPTER 2

The walk to the train station was a lovely one. Blue skies, a slight wet chill in the air that demanded a jumper, and the scent of the sea lingering on the air. It was all Vi would have wanted from the day. She had put a grey jumper over a blue and white sailor dress and put her hair back with a matching blue headband. Jack was dressed in one of his casual suits and with a straw hat. Jack was discussing the possibility of a toffee apple as they moved along. She was pushing the pram as he was simply too tall. He had tried but had been so hunched over he declared that prams were designed by monsters to make fathers suffer.

They had their dogs and Ham's puppies on leashes as they went to get him. Holmes and Rouge trotted along happy and well-trained while Ham's puppies, Watson and Mary, lollygagged to the point that Jack had tucked one under each arm. The sight of him trying to manage all four dogs had her laughing into her hand as they walked to the train station. They'd sent an auto for both of the nannies, Hamilton's things, and Ham, if he preferred, but they intended to walk back.

"Do you want to go fishing?"

He shook his head.

"Do you want to go onto the sea?"

Jack shrugged

"What do you want to do?"

"I—I'm a little worried about Ham. I think he thought Rita would come straight back when he wrote her whatever he did. Instead, she took a trip that lingered at different places, letting her continue to adventure."

Violet didn't bother to point out that Rita wasn't Ham's to beckon and expect her to come trotting up, leash in her mouth, tail wagging. Rita was a full-grown woman who had done more than the rest of the friends combined. She was independent, intelligent, adventurous, and clever. She was a catch for *any* man, and Ham had rejected her love. Did he think Rita had no pride?

Even if she had come back to see if they could work things out, she had to be hesitant. Maybe she'd taken the longer trip back to *force* herself to weigh what she wanted. Maybe she'd needed time to consider him again after spending months trying to get over him.

Violet's mouth twisted at the look on Jack's face. "It isn't going to be easy for either of them."

"I know—" Jack put down Mary and tried to get her to walk at his side again. "By Jove! I know it. I just wish it could be easy for them."

Violet hesitated and then peered down at Agatha and Vivi. "If it were Agatha or Vivi, we would expect someone to earn them. We can't forget that they're *both* our friends. If we do, we'll lose one of them if things—" Vi didn't want to say if things didn't work out. If things didn't work out, she was very much afraid she'd lose Rita as a friend. If things didn't work out, Vi was afraid that Ham would blame her for needling him until they got this far. If things didn't work out, it wouldn't only be Rita and Ham who looked back with regret. Violet, Jack, they all would.

But then again, Violet thought, she would not have married Jack because her friends wanted her too, and Rita deserved the same expectations. As did, Ham. Ham deserved someone who married him because she wanted him.

"I think I'm going to be needing a quiet weekend somewhere else to recover from this quiet weekend," Violet told Jack.

"Me too. Do you know how many times Ham came over when I was tortured over you, and smoked a cigarette or a cigar with me? How many times he poured me a cocktail or a bourbon and just sat there in the quiet? I bet he was dreaming of a time when I would get over you or marry you and he could go back to visiting museums, reading a book, or going dancing. Anything but sitting in the quiet."

"Ahhh," Violet moaned, "that is the *sweetest*. Oh! He's my third favorite bloke—tied with Denny."

Jack's laugh had Violet glancing up at him again, and he asked, "Does your father know he doesn't make your top five men?"

Violet lifted her brows in question, and Jack ticked off, "Me, Victor, Denny, Ham, and Tomas."

She grinned evilly. "I like your dad a lot too. They can be tied for sixth place."

Jack snorted and then picked Mary back up, trying to teach Watson to walk on a leash instead. The train whistle blew in the distance. Ham would be here momentarily. The steamship was supposed to arrive this afternoon, and the passengers and crew were having a farewell party that Rita had begged they attend.

"This should be an interesting day," Jack muttered. The red brick building was just ahead with the weathervane spinning in the wind as if it couldn't quite decide which way the wind was blowing. Vi shivered and leaned down to tuck the blankets closer around the twins, letting her fingers linger on their skin to ensure they were neither too hot nor too cold. Both girls had rosy cheeks, but it didn't seem to stem from the weather, and to the touch they felt quite comfortable. Violet considered for a moment. She'd want the blanket tucked close if she were sleeping outside. She decided to trust her instincts and leave them be.

While she fussed over the babies, the train came rumbling past. It was time to face whatever would happen and make sure that regardless of the outcome, their friendships survived, and they were there for those they loved. She glanced at Jack, who nodded in silent agreement.

"I love you, Mr. Wakefield," she said fondly.

Jack leaned down and pressed a kiss to Violet's forehead and said low and sweet, "I love you, Mrs. Wakefield."

HAM STEPPED off the train in his same old grubby brown suit. She grinned as she saw it and noted that he had seemed to have cut a little more weight, as well as had his hair and beard trimmed. If he weren't wearing the old suit—or its twin, given he was smaller now than when she'd first met him—she'd have teased him about primping for his love. It was in bad taste, she thought, given the tightness to his gaze and the way he moved like he hadn't slept well in days.

"Ham!" Violet called and skipped up to him to press a kiss on his cheek. She'd have taken his briefcase if he'd let her, but he just dropped his own kiss on her forehead where her cloche ended. "It is so nice to see you."

Ham just sort of grunted and then took his dogs from Jack. Both dogs were yipping in excitement at the sight of Ham, and they succeeded where she had not. He grinned at them and rubbed both little grey bellies before he stood.

"We've walked," Jack told him, "and we're having deep, clear thoughts about toffee apples."

Ham stood with his dogs and leaned over the pram to glance at the babies. "They're big now, aren't they?"

"It's too fast," Violet muttered, crossly. "Their grand-mother appropriated more than her fair share of time with them."

Ham laughed again, and his shoulders eased.

"There's an auto, if you'd rather," Jack told Ham. "We promised a long walk to Kate and Victor and must gather up a duo of nannies who are going back to the house to be tried and probably found wanting by Victor."

"He's turned into a grouchy bear," Violet added. "He's

dismissed three *separate* nannies since the girls have arrived."

Ham grunted and Jack clapped him on the back, taking the briefcase from his friend and walking it to the servant who had arrived with the auto. Jack arranged the baggage and nannies while Ham silently smoked a cigarette away from the girls and Violet watched him with concern. He had gone back to tense, and she thought he might need to have someone smack him hard to get it out of him. No one was going to throw herself into the arms of an automaton.

Jack returned with the nannies following. Violet liked the look of Poppy and Jane. She liked their smile lines, the way they laughed back and forth. The way they left the babies sleeping but called them sweet little lambs with such clear-eyed honesty that Violet had little doubt both women adored children. Poppy had rosy cheeks, black and grey hair, a bit of a hook nose, and a wide smile. Jane was a bit quieter and a bit paler, but her face was just as kind and she had more of a button nose.

A quick back and forth established Violet as the aunt, warned them of Victor's protectiveness, and told them a bit about Lila and Denny. Nothing that anyone would object to. "I can take them," Poppy offered.

Violet shook her head quickly. "It's my turn."

Poppy smiled with understanding.

Violet and Jack left the women with the servant and followed Ham out of the train station. Ham walked at a clip that his dogs weren't keeping. Violet didn't bother to chase after Ham. He'd either slow down or take a much-needed ramble before he met Rita again. Instead, Violet followed Jack to the little shop with the toffee apples and they ordered one sliced and to go. When they left the shop, they found Ham smoking outside.

He took one look at them and then said, "I might be bad company."

"We can't all be as wonderful as me," Violet told him consolingly, patting his back.

He grinned at her, and she winked before leaning to pick up the wriggling Agatha. To Ham she said, "In penance, you can push the pram."

Halfway down the first lane, Ham cursed and demanded, "Was this engineered for pixies?"

"This might shock you," Violet whispered, leaning in, "but I suspect it was—in fact—engineered for women."

The wind whipped around them again, and Jack lifted the squirming Vivi. Ham groaned at the four dogs, including his two disobedient ones, and then plopped them in the pram, pushing it and cursing as they headed back to the house they'd taken for the weekend.

The wind whipped away from them across the sea, where the steamship *The Majestic Star* was coming ever closer. How their jaws would have dropped to see Rita staring down in shock at a man on his knee, holding out a makeshift ring with his promises of love.

They would have been *even* more shocked to realize that this was not the blond fellow with the round spectacles that dared to press a kiss on her cheek the night before or the redhead with the wide grin who had slipped a love poem under her door. What would have shocked them all, to their very soul, was the fourth man —watching in the distance, gaze narrowed with hatred as he stared towards the couple with a virulent fury.

# CHAPTER 3

*R*ita had dressed with care. She was wearing a blue sapphire dress that exactly matched the color of her eyes, a long strand of pearls accented by a sapphire and diamond collar, and sapphire and diamond earbobs. Her hair was in marcelled curls with one sapphire hairpin holding them to the side of her face.

Her cosmetics were perfect with a pink lipstick that looked both natural and vibrant. Against her straight white teeth, the color drew attention to every word that dropped from her lips and those pearls were being attended to by no more than four men who circled her.

The steamship's ballroom had a grand staircase that descended into a group of spinning dancers. A band played in the corner that Violet couldn't quite see from her vantage point. There was also a bar along the wall, and doors that led onto the deck were left open for dancers to come and go.

Rita met Violet's gaze, and for a moment, Violet was

sure she'd lost her friend to this last adventure as though they hadn't been friends long enough to last the break, but then Rita shoved past the gents as though they were nothing more than croquet balls in her way. She came darting across the ballroom towards Violet and the others.

"Hullo, hullo, hullo, hullo!" Rita's wide grin was a blur as she threw herself into Violet's arms, hugging her tightly. "Oh! I have missed you so!"

"Umph." Violet squeezed Rita nearly as tightly, breathing in the gardenia and jasmine scent of her friend.

"Well if this isn't one of the prettiest things I've ever seen," a stranger's voice intruded, but Rita didn't let Violet go and neither did Violet. Rita only stepped back when Lila lazily asked, "And where is mine?"

A moment later, the still slim Lila was being hugged tightly. They were whispering into each other's ears, and the sight of her two closest friends together filled Vi's heart with out and out joy.

"All is well again," Rita said delightedly as she repeated, "Hullo, hullo! I've missed you all so! Even Denny!"

Denny grunted, but he was grinning at the sight of his wife hugging their friend. Among the close friends, they were all very carefully *not* looking at Ham. If Rita's gaggle of lovers were watching Ham, Violet didn't dare to look. She wanted so very badly to turn and see his reaction, but as private as he was, he deserved the chance to hide what he was feeling.

Violet grinned at her friends and then turned towards the voice who attempted to interrupt their reunion. It was the first of four men trailing after Rita like ducklings. Oh. Violet barely kept herself from narrowing her gaze and demanding why they were bothering their group.

The man was dark, slim, with a hook nose, and an arrogant manner that rivaled Violet when she was putting on her earl's daughter airs.

"Hello there," the first gent said with a crooked, smarmy grin. His dark gaze flit to Rita and back to Violet. "Lord Parkington Bidlake."

He expected Violet to be impressed. Denny's evil snort had Bidlake turning his head. While he did, Rita winked at Violet who coolly replied, "Lady Violet Wakefield. This is my husband, Jack Wakefield."

Violet never enjoyed using the courtesy title she received from her father except for moments like these. She noticed the rapid blinking as Bidlake reassessed his capacity to impress Rita's friends and then looked beyond him to the other fellows.

"Meet," Rita said merrily, "Oscar Watts."

The blonde with the round spectacles waved.

"Ian Fyfe."

A redhead with the most delightful freckles nodded happily, but Violet noted a bit of anger in his gaze, as though things weren't quite going his way.

"And," Rita said with a wicked grin, "Vernon Atkinson."

The last of the gents, the one who had lagged the most behind, nodded once, not meeting a single person's gaze. He was medium in every way, medium hair, build, color of eyes.

Rita introduced the rest of them in quick succession and without lingering on any one person. Like, Violet thought, Hamilton Barnes. Ham, on the other hand, had clearly examined each of the gents chasing Rita with a dark, judging gaze.

Violet ignored Ham because she thought he'd want her to. Instead, with a merriness that didn't reach her soul, Vi asked Rita, "How was your trip?"

"Oh lovely!" Rita said, hooking her arm with Violet's. She looked at the others apologetically. "I do need to talk to Vi for a moment."

Rita pulled Vi into the crowded ballroom, not bothering to look back at everyone they'd abandoned.

"Jack will understand, right?"

Jack was not Violet's concern.

"They can get drinks," Rita said, knowing they were being rude. She waved towards the bar where drinks could be acquired.

A black woman with a low voice was singing with the accompaniment of a full band, and Rita pulled Violet into a dance. "I—"

Violet lifted a brow.

"I didn't mean to." Her gaze moved to the gents who were staring after Violet and Rita. "They're suffocating."

With a snort, Violet laughed. "It's your natural beauty."

Rita shook her head. "I don't think so. Oh, how that sounds, but no. Somehow rumors of my father's money got out. I had an older woman ask me if my father was that rich bloke Roderick Russell."

"No!" Violet's gaze returned to the gents and she had to wonder which of them was money grubbing. Possibly all of them? Definitely that Bidlake fellow. Certainly, more than just Bidlake, as lovely as Rita was. It was a competition between those fellows, and the prize was likely Rita's money not her heart.

Rita nodded. "I didn't say a word. Ian and Oscar had been flirting before the rumors, but after—"

Violet didn't need Rita to expand. As an heiress herself, Violet knew all too well what happened when a man who was slightly interested realized there was a mountain of gold behind that set of fine eyes or whatever it was they sort of liked.

"Where is Martha? Didn't she help?"

"Oh no. She's in love," Rita said, batting her lashes. "I'm sure she'll be about, and I'll wait for you to see her."

Violet paused at that because there was something in Rita's tone that conveyed that Vi would be surprised by what she saw. Martha was hardly Violet's concern. Lila's little sister was pure, spoiled trouble.

"Tell me more," Violet said and listened to the descriptions of blue seas, fantastical animals, wonderful countries. Temples that left one awestruck, and three separate proposals.

"How did you reply?"

"I said I appreciated each offer but that I wasn't prepared to accept *any* proposal."

Violet was certain the 'any' was for Ham, and she winced. Violet wanted her friend Ham and her friend Rita—who adored each other—to marry each other and find happiness. Ham had, however, flubbed up every-thing when he sidestepped Rita's feelings in order to avoid being seen as pursuing her for her money.

Leaving her open, Violet scowled, for fellows like that Bidlake. Men were so stupid with their pride ruining the good things. Who *cared* if Rita inherited money from her father when her choices were honorable men like Ham, being alone, or ones she couldn't be sure of like those trailing ducklings?

"Don't look at me like that," Rita muttered, pulling Violet towards the side door and out onto the deck where they could talk quietly. "I just—that hurt, Vi."

Kate followed them onto the deck before they could decide between a deckchair or leaning against the railing. Kate hugged Rita tightly. "I know you're avoiding Ham, but I needed my hug too."

"I missed you all so much," Rita murmured. "Adventures aren't the same when home is so appealing."

"You don't have to accept Ham," Kate said before Violet could. "We will love you regardless. You're one of us now. Even to Ham. I know he wants you to feel like you've come home *despite* his feelings for you. Or that his feelings for you are secondary to you being one of us."

Rita looked between them, tears swimming in her eyes. She blinked them quickly away. "That's what I love about him."

Neither Kate nor Violet bothered to ask what Rita didn't like about him. Falling in love and trusting yourself to another was terrifying even before you included the fact that Ham's pride had split them up before. Violet was sure there were a few things about Ham that Rita didn't care for; Violet could certainly think of a thing or two about Jack.

"Vi," Kate cut in. "I saw Martha."

There was *something* in that tone that had Violet staring in surprise at Kate. "Did you?"

"You'll want to as well."

Violet glanced between Kate and Rita, who were both hiding wide, wide grins.

"I don't care for Martha, and I'm sure she's not going anywhere."

"Oh." Rita shook her head. "Actually, I'm sure she'll be leaving soon."

"But there's a party," Violet said, glancing between the two. "The disembarking party. They're famously good fun. With lots of drinks and handsome men."

"Indeed." Rita didn't argue, but somehow that mattered.

"Ham loves you," Violet said fiercely. "You love Ham. We all love you both. Our opinions don't matter."

Rita nodded.

"Do what you need to do, except for Bidlake. You're going to need to not end up with him despite the proposals."

"He's a good dancer," Rita told Violet simply.

"That doesn't extend to day-to-day life."

"I know," Rita admitted and her wicked grin had Violet grinning in return. "But the ship stopped so many places, and there were so many evenings of dancing to be filled. Oscar is a sweetie and so is Vernon, but their dancing leaves something to be desired."

"Your toes?"

"I wanted to walk on the beaches of the islands where we stopped and dive into the deep end of the pool without a flash of pain."

"She's demanding, isn't she?" Violet asked Kate, who yawned into her gloved hand and then nodded.

"I'm sorry. Babies—"

"Oh, I am so excited to see them. I bought all of the

baby things I saw, I think."

Kate hugged Rita again and then said, "Really Vi. Lila needs you, I think."

SLOWLY VIOLET STARTED BACK towards the ballroom where she'd abandoned her other friends. As she searched for Jack's head towering over the rest, Violet paused. In front of Jack was a slender woman wearing a very simple, very stark black dress. Her blonde hair was pulled back into a low barrette, far outside of fashion. Given that it had been bobbed the last time that Violet had seen Martha, she must have been trying to grow it longer since she left. Next to her was a man in all black, wearing a *collar*.

"Is that…"

"Brother Samuel Richards," Rita murmured. "Just returning to England to raise more funds for his next mission. He joined us a few stops from where the ship started, from this tiny island. It seemed he was doing good works there, but—"

Violet's jaw dropped as the woman next to him turned slightly and Vi noticed Martha wasn't wearing any cosmetics. No! Then Vi noticed the look of disgust and irritation on Lila's face. Violet hurried across the ballroom, abandoning Rita and Kate.

As Vi arrived she heard Martha said, "Like the good book says, a virtuous woman is valuable above rubies."

"Like Vi says," Denny said loudly. His disgusted look was only slightly eased when Victor thrust a cocktail into his friend's hand and then handed over his own cigarette.

"Ah, brother Denny," Samuel said, "that *is* indeed a

scripture. Though, of course, Martha has misquoted it slightly. It says, of course, "Who can find a virtuous woman? For her price *is* far above rubies. The heart of her husband doth safely trust in her, so that he shall have no need of spoil. She will do him good and not evil all the days of her life."

Violet blinked at Denny, whose mouth had dropped open. He was gaping like a fish as he stared at the fellow Martha was clinging to.

From behind them, Violet added, "She seeketh wool, and flax, and worketh *willingly,*" Violet's gaze was intent as she stared at Martha, "with her hands."

Denny's evil snort combined with Violet's quote had Martha blushing furiously. She turned and the circle of friends widened to allow Violet, Kate, and Rita to enter.

"Yes, yes, of course," Samuel said, holding out a hand to Violet. "How right you are, sister."

"Violet is fine," Violet told him. He was handsome. Shockingly so. Tanned from the island, with blue eyes and dark hair, it was an arresting combination.

"Sister Violet—"

"Just Violet," she cut in with a smile.

His smarmy smile lessened his looks dramatically. "Are we not all sisters and brothers, children of God?"

"We are indeed," Violet said quickly, "but I am afraid that I only accept the title of sister from Victor. The rest of mankind will need to use my name." It was a firm order, and he attempted to stare her down, again lessening his looks. He'd gone from attractive to repellent with just a few words.

"Of course sister…ah, Violet, if it makes you uncomfortable."

"It does." Violet took his hand, squeezed it once, and then took Jack's arm. She didn't bother glancing up at her husband's face, but she had little doubt that it was filled with quiet amusement.

In the break, Denny added, "What I meant, *of course,* was that though that phrase is a scripture, *Martha* learned it from Violet. *Not from study.*"

Martha's gaze narrowed on Denny. Her glance was hate-filled before she looked up at *Brother* Samuels with a saccharine sweet expression.

"Of course, of course, sis—ah, Violet is clearly a great studier of scripture. A virtuous woman. I am sure your husband has no fear of you."

Victor snorted and Lila choked back a laugh while Bidlake and Denny laughed out hard. Jack shifted slightly as Violet saw red. Before Vi could find anything to say, Martha tried simpering up at Brother Samuel.

He said, "I'm sure you're aware that Martha is a willing student of God's word. I find her to be a bit like a hummingbird, don't you? Her attention is hard to keep, but she is a fine and delicate creature, created by the Lord to be shepherded, guided, and safeguarded."

Violet's fingers dug into Jack's arm and no one had a reply to Samuel except Martha, who gazed up at him with besotted eyes as she said, "Of course, of course."

"Bloody hell," Denny muttered. "I didn't think she could get worse. Victor, I need another drink. Something stronger."

Victor muttered something low and pulled Kate after him as they went towards the bar.

"Whatever happened to your gaggle of lovers, Rita?" Ham asked as only Bidlake had remained behind. He sounded just irritated enough for his feelings to be evident, but then he cleared his throat as he met her gaze. "I'm sorry. I shouldn't have said anything. It's nice to see you again."

The words were so starkly not all he wanted to say that it seemed as if the rest of them could feel them in the air. His love was there, however, in his gaze, his expression, the way his head tilted and his eyes moved anxiously over her to ensure that all was well.

What surprised no one was how Rita seemed to be doing the same. Her gaze moved over Ham with quick little movements that checked that he was also well. What was even more fascinating was the way that Bidlake followed both of their gazes. He might have been obtuse when it came to thinking he could slap out a title and have people awed. However, he wasn't at all imperceptive when it came to being aware of Rita.

"I've heard you've been doing good work," Rita said to Ham, attempting merry and failing. She sounded as though something were caught in her throat. "Catching killers. Making the world safer."

Ham didn't answer until Jack nudged him. "Oh yes, I —suppose. You know, same as usual with these ones about. Jack doing half the detecting. Violet meddling and discovering things she shouldn't. We've a new friend, Jovie. You'll like her, I think."

"That's what Vi said," Rita started, but Bidlake cleared his throat and then cut into the conversation.

"It's good to have those plebian working souls about, don't you think, Rita?"

Rita's gaze narrowed and she shot a nasty look towards Bidlake, but he was too busy looking triumphantly at Ham and Denny to even realize he'd infuriated Rita.

Denny held up his hands at Bidlake. "Don't look at me, boyo. I'm neither a good worker nor Rita's lover. If, however, you think that insulting her family will gain you her heart, you're dumber than you seem."

Bidlake pretended to laugh before he scowled at Samuels. "What are you doing here? I told you I wouldn't be donating to your futile mission."

"He's here with me," Martha hissed. "You're the interloper."

"Now, now, always kind, Sister Martha," Samuels said, making Denny groan again and look at Lila with a plea.

"The railing is so close," he told her.

"And why are you here?" Bidlake muttered to Martha. "No one wants you about either. Pretended right-eousness is even more irksome than projected right-eousness."

"Oh man," Denny said, eating an olive off of his martini. "I wanted to hate him."

"You still can," Ham said and Denny guffawed. Neither of them were bothered when Bidlake seemed offended.

Bidlake tried to laugh. "I didn't think your friends were religious. Why do you have these ones about?"

"We believe in God," Lila told him lazily. "He's clearly smiting us now for what we've done. I blame Denny's gluttony."

"I don't understand," Samuel said, glancing between Violet's friends.

"There, there," Lila told him. "Why would you?"

"Lila!" Martha scolded in a hissed whisper. "Stop it!"

To Samuel, Martha said, "She's teasing you, Brother Samuel."

"Did she call him brother?" Denny demanded, looking to Jack for confirmation.

"She did," Jack and Ham agreed.

Victor turned to Kate. "Dance with me before I sick up."

"Does the good word offend?" Samuel asked, glancing at Martha for an answer. "Does the good word make him ill?"

"He doesn't like the way Brother Bidlake was talking about working souls," Martha lied smoothly. "Victor, like all my friends, is spoiled but good. You'll see. Once you look past their flaws, they're exactly the kind of people to help finance our missionary work."

"Our?" Lila snapped.

"Brother Samuel and I are going to wed," Martha told her sister triumphantly before she slapped a pious expression back on her face.

"She did it again," Denny told Lila. "She called him brother. Make it stop or it won't just be Victor sicking up."

Lila stared between Martha and Samuel and then said lazily, "I'll pay for your next five years of missionary work if you leave my sister alone."

"I'll help with that," Violet shot out.

"Me too," Rita agreed.

"Lila!" Martha shrieked, not whispering.

"We'll make it twenty years if you leave before morning," Denny added. He really did look sick to his stomach. "And if we never hear you use the terms 'brother' or 'sister' again."

Brother Samuel looked between the friends and then faced Martha. "Maybe it's for the best."

She stared at him, jaw dropping open. "Are you shamming me?"

"Sister Martha, we must put the good work first."

"But—"

"Think of the good I could do."

"But we could get donations from other people," she tried, tears welling in her eyes.

Violet winced. She thought that Martha might actually be heartbroken. The look on her face was devastating until Violet followed Martha's gaze to the man who'd thrown her over in a moment, publicly, for money.

"Not for twenty years," Brother Samuel told her regretfully. "I trust that the good work we've done on your soul will continue. I will pray for you."

She gasped.

"I will look back at you with fondness."

Martha asked slowly, "What do you mean?"

"Sister Martha, I was never convinced...."

Her gaze narrowed.

"God must come first."

Martha slapped him hard.

"If you give him one half-penny," she said crossly to Lila, Violet, and Rita, "I'll never forgive you!"

"Deal," Denny said for the rest of them. "Go away Brother Samuel, before we toss you over the side of the boat for playing with the emotions of our hideous Martha."

At that, Martha wailed and ran from the room. With a sigh, Lila followed.

# CHAPTER 4

*V*iolet knocked on Rita's bedroom door early the next morning and found her friend already dressed and sitting near the window of their rented house. Vi, Rouge, and Holmes entered Rita's room and Vi curled up on the bed and looked at Rita. Rouge leapt onto the bed with Violet, but her newer spaniel, Holmes, joined Rita.

"Don't say it." Rita didn't even look up, so she didn't see the box of chocolates waving in the air between the two of them until Vi groaned.

Rita took in the embossed box, wrapped in amethyst ribbon.

Violet handed Rita the box of chocolates that Violet's newest business partner, Mariposa Jenkins, had sent just before Violet and Jack had left their London house. Rita opened it and breathed them in, noting the gold decoration painted on a few of the chocolates. There was one with a pistachio on top because Mariposa refused to let the events that occurred after she met Violet ruin her love of pistachios. Violet's favorite was the small rose made of swirled white and dark chocolate.

Violet had invested in Mariposa Jenkins because Vi believed in the woman. A single mother who was working hard and continuously for her children deserved a little help. The periodic box of chocolates to show what Mariposa was doing was unexpected and welcome.

Rita sighed as she took a truffle from the box. "Am I sabotaging my happiness by not...not...leaping into his arms and swearing my eternal love?"

"The fact that you're here is something of a sign," Violet said carefully.

Rita glanced up and then popped the pistachio chocolate into her mouth. "It's not enough, is it?"

"What if you were honest?"

"I haven't lied," Rita snapped.

"What if you told Ham that your feelings were hurt?"

"Then he'd know." Rita frowned fiercely down at her twisted hands.

"If you think he wasn't destroyed by you leaving, you're wrong," Violet told Rita. "He disappeared on case after case for a while and even still—it's not like it's been cigars, dancing, and cocktails. It hasn't. My goodness, I bought him dogs to cheer him up."

Rita looked unaffected.

"He lost weight because he had no appetite."

Still nothing.

"I know you were hurt. I understand, believe me. Jack and I didn't just fall into each other's arms, and there was a fair amount of thinking I was going to love him from afar forever. That I'd either be alone for the rest of my life, looking onto Victor's children—poisonously jealous—only to eventually settle for someone like that Bidlake fellow."

Rita's mouth twisted and she huffed a little before clucking to Holmes until the dog crawled into her lap and began licking her chin.

"I just think you should tell him how he made you feel. Let him say whatever he is going to say and then determine if his response is something you can live with. Especially given how you *love him* and he *loves you*."

Rita nodded, deliberately not replying, and stood, carrying Holmes with her. "You look nice, by the way."

Vi looked down at her sapphire blue day dress and tan t-strap shoes and then at Rita who was wearing a powder blue dress that was cut nearly exactly the same. Vi winked at Rita and followed her down the stairs for the breakfast room. Violet saw Rita pause as she hit the doorway and then heard, "Good morning, Hamilton."

Instead of going in, Violet sidestepped to head down the hall towards the back patio with the intent of giving them some time. Before she got more than one step, she heard Rita say, "I—didn't intend on all those gents—that just happened."

Ham's reply was too low to hear, but Violet heard Rita laugh.

"I missed you," Ham replied a little louder and Violet felt a burning at the back of her eyes. She prayed silently that things would work out between them. "I—"

She turned when she heard the creak of a step behind her and found none other than the red-headed fellow from the steamship.

"Hello there," he said to Violet, who narrowed her gaze. He saw her expression, but ignored it when he asked, "I was wondering if Rita was available?"

Vi looked beyond him to the front door, wondering who allowed him to make his way through their house when she saw a furiously red-faced maid, wringing her hands, shooting dark looks towards Ian Fyfe.

"Did you just push past the maid?"

A flush crossed Ian's face, but he cleared his throat and repeated, "Rita? Rita Russell? She's staying here. The boy who delivered her bags from the ship told me she was."

Because Violet had moved from irritated to furious she demanded, "So you bribed a servant to provide you information that Rita didn't give you herself?"

"I'm sure it was just an oversight."

"Or she didn't want you showing up during breakfast," Violet snapped. "What are you trying to do? Beat the other boys out of the gates?"

The blush had become brilliant. "Would you just get Rita?"

"She's in there," Violet told him smoothly as she nodded at the doorway only a few steps beyond, giving him a quiet, evil grin. They were close enough that Rita couldn't have missed their conversation.

The look of fury in his eyes was enough that Violet grinned cheekily. The low curse word he muttered wasn't loud enough for Rita to hear, but Violet wasn't going to be playing games. And if she was, she'd be playing a dirty trick if necessary. Violet was on Ham's side.

She waited until he stepped into the breakfast room and then asked loudly, "Did you just call me a —"

Rita gasped as Violet followed. Ham met Violet's gaze, and she saw that same quiet humor in his gaze that matched Jack. They might be years apart in age and unrelated, but they were the same in so many ways. You had to know them to know when they were amused, and at the moment, Ham was holding back a guffaw.

"Who called you that word?" Victor asked from behind Violet and then stepped into the room. "This bloke?"

Ian Fyfe held up his hands in surrender, starting to explain, but Victor grabbed Ian by the back of the neck.

"Hey now," Ian said, trying to squirm away.

But Victor had the look of a man woken a half-dozen times by his twin daughters. Victor shoved the protesting Ian toward the door and told the maid, "Just don't answer it until we're done with breakfast. It seems Rita's money-grubbing lovers have forgotten their manners in their greed."

The maid opened the door just in time for Victor to toss out Ian, slam the door closed, and lock it. Violet bit down on her bottom lip as Victor turned. They'd left the breakfast room to watch Ian tossed curbside.

"What?"

"You look tired," Violet told him. Her wicked grin could not be held back.

Victor glanced at the maid. "Not your fault, Jenny."

She nodded and darted down the hallway as Victor continued. "Being this tired is worse now. We'd found that level of sleep exhaustion that was familiar. Getting

34

sleep and then having it snatched back away is perhaps worse than it was before."

"Didn't two nannies arrive yesterday?" Ham asked carefully. He took Rita's arm and backed up as though Victor were rabid.

"I don't know Poppy and Jane well enough yet to know how they'll be when they're woken in the middle of the night. Couldn't be risked."

The four of them moved towards the breakfast room the moment they realized they were standing in the hall for no reason. Violet crossed to the coffee pot and poured her brother a Turkish coffee and then returned for her refill.

Victor looked between Rita and Ham. "Rita, Ham missed you. Ham, I'm sure Rita missed you too. She came back after all. You both love each other, and those blokes are after Rita's money. Given that she's beautiful too, they must feel like they found the pot of gold at the end of the rainbow."

Both Rita and Ham were staring at him as Violet sat down next to her twin and popped him on the back of the head. "He's tired."

"I'll tell you one thing that I always hated when folks told me. Life really is better when you are married to someone you love. Don't be stupid and think they're wrong." Victor sniffed and then swallowed a large, too-hot gulp of coffee, and then groaned.

"Are you done?" Violet demanded.

Victor nodded.

"He's tired," Violet repeated to Ham and Rita and then with the echo of her slow, evil grin from earlier she added, "but he's right."

Rita pressed her lips together. "I didn't intend to become the hunted heiress on the steamship. And, I don't know—there's more to like to me than money, right?"

"Right," Violet and Ham said instantly.

Victor pursed his mouth and looked Rita over as though he were judging a horse at a fair. Violet smacked the back of his head again and then said to Rita, "He's still tired."

"I am tired," Victor agreed. "You're pretty great, Rita. It's not everyone who would search hotel rooms with Violet and follow her into trouble. You know, other than all of our friends."

"I wouldn't," Ham admitted.

"Jack wouldn't either." Violet considered breakfast and then decided that fruit and toast was just what she needed. She rose to make up a plate as Jack appeared. He had gotten up early and gone for a walk. He stepped into the room with just a bit of red in his cheeks from his walk.

"There's a fellow outside the house who is pacing and cursing. The redheaded one. I remember you telling me his name, Rita, but I do not recall caring about what it was. The other one, with the spectacles, is there too. He seems to think it's all very funny. Especially when I had to circle the house and go in the servant's entrance."

Rita sniffed and sipped her tea as if she were completely unbothered.

"That Ian fellow is no longer welcome in the house," Victor said. "If Rita goes for him—"

"I won't," Rita replied, giving Victor a nasty look. "Violet told me I couldn't go for Bidlake either."

"Well in that case—" Jack started but Rita's nasty

glance and Violet's quick shake of the head had him saying instead, "I'm glad you're back, Rita."

Violet was utterly unsurprised when Victor winked at Rita and then handed Violet his coffee cup. She refilled it for him even though she normally would have snapped at him.

Violet looked back at her friends and then crossed to Jack instead of Victor, taking her seat next to him and laying her head on his shoulder. "What if we were to go to the carnival tonight? The pier and the carnival both look like a fun way to spend the evening."

Rita winced. "In order to sidestep giving out my address, I told Bidlake that I'd be attending the carnival this evening when he said they were having an adult-only session after 8:00 p.m. this evening."

"You would be," Violet shot back, "with us."

Rita knew Violet's wicked tone of voice, but she just shook her head and said, "I suppose I would be."

"I'm happy to throw him out of the house for you as well," Victor said. "Or out of the carnival or off the pier. Whatever you need."

"We're really service-oriented friends," Violet told Rita brightly.

THE REST of breakfast passed peacefully until, at least, Lila's little sister, Martha, entered. She looked as though she'd cried the evening over, but she'd set aside the simple black dress for a soft pink dress that showed her shoulders and dipped low over her chest. Violet rose to get Martha a cup of English breakfast tea after taking in the real circles under the younger woman's eyes.

Martha sniffed and sat down, staring at the table.

"Come now," Victor told Martha gently, "it isn't so bad."

"I really loved Samuel," Martha said, "and—and—he threw me over for money."

"He did," Victor agreed, "which means that he wasn't the man you thought he was, and he didn't have the feelings for you that he pretended."

Martha stared at Victor as though she'd never thought of that idea. Really, Violet thought, how could Martha be quite so dim when Lila was so clever?

"He wasn't, was he? He talked so nicely. I thought a missionary would be better than these regular gents. Like that Bidlake. He was interested enough in me when the ship departed until he found out that Rita was an heiress."

"Samuel thought you could get him money," Violet said nearly as gently as Victor, though she *had* noted what Martha had said about Bidlake.

Martha fought to hold back the tears again. "I thought I was going to be married. I thought I'd get a pretty dress and we'd have a big party. How happy Mama would have been when I married a missionary. That's way better than lazy Denny!"

Violet tucked her hair behind her ear to fight her reaction.

"Are you sadder about the wedding or the man?" Rita's dry voice said she'd long since run out of sympathy for Martha.

Vi met Rita's gaze and bit down on her bottom lip. It

wasn't as though they hadn't warned Rita. She just hadn't cared when she needed to get away from Ham.

"Well." Martha frowned and then she brightly said, "It's not like I won't find someone else. I'm pretty and now that we're off that steamship where everyone around wants Rita's money, I'll have a better chance. It's really unfair that you're so fashionable *and* that you have so much money."

"No one wants to be married for their money," Rita snapped. "Whether it's money for the missionary work or money for parties and suits."

Martha scowled at Rita, crossing her arms over her chest. "It's not *fair* that Rita is both pretty and rich," she said again, but this time with more whining in her voice.

"Life isn't fair," Violet told Martha.

"You're pretty and rich too. You just matter less because you're already married."

Victor choked on his coffee while Violet stared, open-mouthed. She'd jumped ahead with the shock, though, because then Martha said, "If only I had a rich aunt who was murdered and left me everything."

"I say!" Ham snapped while Jack slowly set down his coffee cup. Rita's gasp was followed by Victor's low growl.

Violet rose with a look for Victor. "I've got this one."

Crossing to Martha, Violet took the girl by the ear and pulled her from the breakfast room. She was twisting until Violet took her by the neck as well, letting her fingernails dig in a bit. Violet calmly walked Martha up the stairs to her bedroom, opened the door, and shoved her in.

"It is untenable that you've made light of my aunt's murder," Violet said evenly.

"I didn't—"

Violet held up a hand and her cool voice snapped as she said, "You did. And you know you did. You may rejoin us this evening if you are prepared to keep a civil tongue in your mouth and apologize clearly. Otherwise, I will put you on a train, send you home to your mother, and chase your exit with a letter regarding your behavior."

"I am a grown woman, and you cannot treat me like a child!"

"Are you? I hadn't noticed." Violet closed the door, locking Martha in. The girl began shaking the handle and demanding to be let out. Violet was certain the only reason she hadn't had to shove Martha back was that the girl didn't think she'd get locked in.

She had always been stupid, Vi thought as she crossed to Lila's bedroom door and banged on it. Denny answered, looking beyond Violet to Martha's door where the pounding against it hadn't stopped.

"I thought all my dreams had come true," Denny said with his gaze still fixed across the hall.

Violet tucked the key into his palm. "She bemoaned not having a rich, murdered aunt."

"I say." Denny's gaze flit to Violet to see her reaction.

Her white-faced fury was a precise answer. "I told her to apologize and change her behavior or we'd put her on the train. You can decide when she can leave the room."

Violet patted Denny's cheek and then left as the sound of something breaking crashed against the floor.

Denny was almost gleeful as he called out to Martha, "That doesn't sound like an apology."

Her shriek of fury had him giggling. He crossed to the door and knocked on it. In a sing-song voice, he called, "Martha…you're a child."

She pounded on the door in answer. "Let me out!"

"Apologize!"

"I'm tired of being treated like a child!"

"Then stop throwing tantrums! You're a horrendous brat!"

"I hate you!"

"I hate you," he called back, laughing. "Always have."

"Oh, oh, oh! I'm going to tell Mother."

Denny's wicked laughter won the argument.

# CHAPTER 5

*T*he traveling carnival was set up near the seaside. The path towards the entrance was lined with torches. They had turned onto the path and Vi paused long enough to enjoy the flicker of the shadows on the pebble walk. The sound from the carnival was filled with laughter and music, and Violet hoped there would be a place to dance.

Her arm was hooked through Jack's and Lila walked next to them. Both Violet and Lila had opted for dresses without sleeves and jumpers that could be tied around the neck or worn depending on how crowded the carnival got or how cool the evening became.

Rita had hurried a dozen steps ahead, excited as they'd left the house. "There is something magical about a carnival. I remember my first one in India. It wasn't the same as here, of course, but I did get to eat samosas and ride an elephant. My mother had a little monkey that adored her and followed her the whole evening, but I suspect it was because she fed it. She swore, however, it was magic."

"That sounds magical," Ham told her. His gaze followed Rita as though she were a unicorn in the distance—surreal, impossible, and just out of reach.

Violet watched Ham watch Rita and then glanced up at Jack. She was arrested for a moment at the look in his eyes. "What?"

Lila laughed and Vi turned to meet her friend's gaze.

"He's looking at you like Ham looks at Rita."

"Denny only looks at chocolate like that," Martha said, "so now you know where you fall, Lila."

Vi gasped but Denny cut in, "The key here, Martha, is that no one will look at you if you keep on being a poisonous wretch."

Rita sighed as they saw five men lingering at the entrance to the carnival. Bidlake held a bouquet of flowers, Ian Fyfe held a box of chocolates, Oscar Watts held a small rectangular box, and Vernon Atkinson held a bottle of champagne.

"Your hands are going to be full," Martha said sourly. Her own gaze was fixed on Samuel Richards, who held nothing at all in his hands. "Could we please carry on? I am ready to dance and drink and ride that carousel."

"Oh Martha," Samuel said in disappointment, glancing her over. She was wearing a red, fringed dress that danced just above her knees, long glass beads around her throat, and she'd applied her cosmetics carefully. The biggest change was, however, the bob she had reinstituted while locked in her bedroom. "You didn't even last one day on God's path without a shepherd."

Martha bypassed Samuel, accepted her ticket from

Ham, and entered through the gates with Samuel following her. Martha was, however, the only one who hurried ahead. The rest lined up and watched as Rita's slew of lovers jockeyed to go first. Vernon stepped up while Bidlake and Fyfe were staring each other down.

"Rita, I wonder if I might steal part of your evening." He smiled charmingly, adjusting his tie with the champagne tucked under his arm.

"Thank you for the very kind offer," Rita started.

Vernon's smile shifted from charming to triumphant.

"—but, I have plans this evening."

"Rita, darling, I only have so much time in Felixstowe, before I have to get back to my regular obligations. Surely, you know I am expecting an answer to a certain question."

Rita glanced at her eager audience, winced, and then said, "I'll find you later if I can. But I came with these friends and have already agreed to have a dance with Lord Bidlake."

Vernon's smile disappeared and Violet had to bite down on her bottom lip as he scowled, chucked the champagne aside, and went into the carnival.

"Why didn't he just leave?" Violet demanded under her breath. "Why is he going to a carnival after being turned down?"

"That's a lot of money on the line," Denny muttered. "Even a man of my high principles would be tempted to declare love for that bullion. And it isn't as though Rita is repugnant. A girl as lovely as Rita who is also wealthy? That's worth rolling with a rejection."

Lila shook her head. "For as often as fellows attempt to marry a girl for their money, it isn't as though it's so easy as they make it seem. We're not lined up like apples at market."

"Apples?" Jack asked.

Violet laughed and then they all shut up in unison as Bidlake pushed ahead of Fyfe, which only infuriated him further. Ian Fyfe, was red-faced, squint-eyed, and ready to blow up.

Jack tensed enough for Violet to become even more alarmed. Fyfe shoved back in and said, "Rita! I—"

"I heard what you said to my friend," Rita told him flatly, ignoring Bidlake to deal with Ian Fyfe.

"You don't understand—"

"Don't I?"

It wasn't possible for Fyfe to blush deeper. "She was baiting me! Trying to trap me!"

"Whatever are you talking about? She forced that word from you? I hardly think so. In fact, I hardly think any *gentleman* would use the term regardless of what the object of his dislike was doing."

Ian's hands fisted as he demanded furiously, "Why are you taking her side? Why would you trust her over me?"

"Because she's my dearest friend," Rita shot back. "Of course I trust her over a man I've known for a few weeks."

"She wants you to end up with that...that...idiot Barnes."

Violet's nails dug into Jack's forearm, and her gaze jumped to Hamilton, who was entirely unaffected. "He's not worried."

Jack laughed silently, but Violet felt the vibration of it against her arm. "Ham doesn't need to worry about that fellow even before Fyfe insulted you. I don't think he needs to worry about any of these fellows."

Violet watched Ham. His close-cut beard hid the little twitches of his mouth that would have given Jack away. If anything, he seemed as though he were waiting in line. Not particularly bothered, not particularly excited.

Violet believed his performance almost as much as she believed Fyfe's protestations of love.

"What's all this now?"

A couple in their middle years watched the group of younger people carefully and then said, "Fyfe? Ian Fyfe? Whatever are you doing in Felixstowe? I thought you were to catch the train to Edinburgh the moment the ship landed?"

"None of your business, Martin. Keep your nose to your own self."

"Why are you bothering this young woman? Your father isn't going to like hearing of this."

"Keep to your own self!" Ian shouted. "Bloody hell man, can't you see this is my girl?"

"Here now," Bidlake muttered.

"She's my girl," Violet announced. "We're making a scene. Rita, darling, I hear that the toffee apple man has a stand in the carnival today."

"I like toffee apples," Rita said, glancing in near apology to Bidlake and Oscar Watts before she side-stepped Fyfe with Violet. "My heavens, I hadn't seen that side of Ian before. He *hates* you, Vi."

"At least Victor and Kate decided to stay home with the babies. Your lover might have attacked Victor. Then I would have had to bring out my mean face."

Vi glanced behind her and found Ham and Jack trailing. They'd have seemed like nursemaids except they both had their wolf faces on. All protective and aware. Vi watched Ham's gaze dart to several drunken young men before he took two steps forward and casually blocked them getting closer to Rita and Vi.

"Where's Denny and Lila?"

"Denny saw a chocolatier."

Rita snorted, sidestepping a girl with her arms full of prizes and her trailing lover. "The best things never change. Oh, look!"

Violet followed Rita's casual pointing. It was Samuel Richards talking quietly to two large men. They were nodding as he spoke quickly to them, and Violet would have guessed he was giving the fellows orders if there was the slightest chance that the blokes were parishioners. What *was* he doing? Asking for donations? Trying to convert carnival goers in their frivolity? Surely he knew the best time to catch someone for the Lord was when they were regretting their life choices, not when they were in the midst of making them. Finding those fellows hungover and sick the next morning with a couple of aspirin and the good word? Perhaps.

"What an odd man he is," Violet murmured to Rita. "Did you get to know him well on the steamship?"

Rita shook her head. "He definitely seemed to move among the passengers. Spent an odd amount of time with Bidlake, to be honest. I was always surprised by that, but avoided them when they were together. Ian spent a good amount of time with Richards too, but Ian also spent a lot of time with some of the sailors, with one of the mates—perhaps the second? Honestly, we were all in each other's pockets so much that we had to *try* to avoid each other to be successful at it."

"Fyfe doesn't seem like a man who would be willing to avoid anyone. Better that they avoid him." Ham's comment wasn't negative and Rita faced him in surprise. She had a low-level blush running and Violet was guessing it was due to the sheer presence of Ham. What if Vi and Jack faded into the crowd and left the two of them together?

Vi looked at Jack and he shook his head at her. Her gaze narrowed, and he shook his head again. Darn him! His preternatural ability to guess what she was thinking was irritating indeed. "If we're going to a carnival—"

"And we are," Rita added.

"Then we must eat fairy floss, ride the carousel, and play one of those tossing things games." Violet lifted a brow in challenge at Rita, knowing that Jack would be happy with whatever they chose to do. He'd already told her that he wanted to walk along the shore, go fishing on the ocean, and visit an old friend in Ipswich. Beyond that, he was willing to be pleased.

"I wonder if we can find a place to ride horses on the beach." Rita's gaze was on the costumed white horses performing near the center of the carnival. "Look at those magnificent creatures."

They watched for several minutes and were interrupted by Victor appearing behind them. "Hullo, hullo."

Violet glanced up and lifted a brow.

"Kate fell asleep. The nannies told me unequivocally to leave them be or else, and I thought—'well, I could, couldn't I?' So I did. I just put on a suit and left the house and to be honest, I feel as though I might be able to fly."

Jack's laugh had Victor shooting him a dark look. "Just wait until you have a little creature who can't even lift their head without depending upon you. You'll be as anxious as I have been."

"What convinced you to trust Poppy and Jane?" Violet didn't believe for a minute that being ordered away by the nannies would have persuaded Victor if he truly didn't trust them.

"Smith's report on those old girls. He's a shady fellow. He followed them, watched them with other children, snuck into their rooms. He even took note of what they ate. How did he find that? But I'll tell you what, that Poppy drinks an excessive amount of tea, but the old girl didn't just take care of her own charges, she was found protecting and looking after other tots too."

"Finish it," Violet told him.

Victor grinned. "Smith said—and I quote, 'Should I ever have the misfortune of being overcome by progeny, I'd do what I could to hire these old broads myself.' I figured if a fellow like Smith would trust them, why shouldn't I?"

"You don't think he has lesser standards?" Ham asked. "Being half-way to a criminal?"

"I think if anyone would see the worst in someone, it's a shady bloke like Smith. That report about set my heart alight. Even Kate agrees."

Violet bit down on her bottom lip to hide a wide grin at that. Kate wanted a nanny, and she wasn't nearly so paranoid in her judgement of her fellow man. Victor saw a devil behind every pair of knitting needles. Kate was far more rational.

"I see that smirk, Vi."

Violet pasted an innocent expression on her face, but he knew her too well.

"Just wait."

The dire warning had no effect. For what? A baby? She wasn't quite ready to delve into motherhood, but when the day arrived, she'd be stealing Poppy or Jane or finding their equivalent.

"Oh," Rita said, and Vi saw Lord Bidlake watching them. "I had better…I did promise…please, excuse me."

Rita avoided Ham's gaze, and then crossed to Bidlake who held out an arm and put on a smile even though he had to be perturbed by her abandoning him earlier. Vi noted the lack of roses and guessed he hadn't been able to keep his temper any more than Vernon Atkinson, the medium brown, medium height lover who'd shown a not so medium temper.

# CHAPTER 6

"*W*ell, wasn't that awkward and uncomfortable?" Victor's voice was gleeful, reminding Vi of the fact that Denny and Victor had long since been the best of friends. Victor slapped Ham on the back, and demanded, "Where is Martha? I do need some good entertainment."

"You missed it already," Ham told Victor. "How about a pint instead?"

Victor followed Ham into the tent serving what smelled like very bad beer.

"We've been abandoned," Violet said to Jack.

"I guess that means we'll have to entertain ourselves."

"Dancing?"

"Indubitably," he told her, not hiding his grin, and he elbowed his way towards the 'dance floor' with the band on a raised platform to one side. The singer was better than Vi would have imagined. The fellow was older than what was common, but the songs were good and so was the band. They spun through the dances, catching sight of Martha in Ian Fyfe's arms and Denny spinning with Lila. Later, they found Victor dancing with one of the acrobats, and Ham stealing a dance with Rita while Bidlake glared daggers.

"Do you really think that Rita didn't intend to come back with all these lovers?" Jack's muse made Violet grin.

"I think at least one of them was purposeful or at least, sort of welcomed with a bit of revenge."

Jack winced. Rita had returned to dancing with Bidlake and she was smiling happily enough, but Ham seemed unconcerned as he and Victor smoked on the sidelines of the dancing area. Neither of the men were looking towards Rita twirling in Bidlake's arms, and there wasn't a deliberateness to it either. Instead, it seemed that Victor was telling a tale, and Ham was amused enough to attend to Victor's story.

The night seemed to prance on, and Violet watched a tumbling act of clowns as she held onto Jack's shoulder so she could see past the giants in front of them. They danced again and found Martha and Samuel, holding hands and speaking quietly.

"Oh dear," Violet muttered.

"Don't lose faith in Martha," Jack told Vi. "Look at her eyes."

Violet looked again and noticed the way Martha's gaze was following a particularly handsome man, and then how she peered up at Samuel and murmured something low to him. He patted her hands and leaned in, and Martha shifted to the side.

How things had turned, Vi thought. From pursuer to pursued and reveling in it.

"I both despise and adore her," Violet told Jack. "But I do really want her to move on from us. How do we rid ourselves of her and still keep Lila and Denny?"

"Marrying her off would be just the thing," Jack answered, "but dislike her as I do, I can't stomach seeing her with that fellow. He had her completely changed, and she wasn't even happy. I believe people can change, Vi, but I do think those changes need to be internally driven."

"It was all an act," Violet told him. "Martha was probably telling herself to bag the man and then convince him to stay in England, and then convince him to take a job with someone or other, and then to take her dancing. I don't believe for a second that she intended to follow him back to some distant island and do good works."

Jack and Violet spun back into the dancing, and a few minutes later, Ian Fyfe requested to break in.

"Surely you must be joking." Violet had little desire to dance with the man, and her reply had him flushing. Violet guessed that flush wasn't embarrassment but anger.

His reply, however, was pleading. "Rita will never let me talk to her until I apologize to you, and I did behave very badly."

Violet tilted her head as she examined him. She didn't want to make amends with him, and she didn't want to dance with him, but she did want him to go away. He didn't know Rita well enough to know that he wouldn't be able to just tell her that he told Violet he was sorry therefore Rita should pretend as though it had never happened.

Violet would like to believe that few modern women

were so foolish as to believe that nonsense, but she knew that more than a few had. Rita, however, was not one of them. If anything, a half-hearted apology that would no doubt be chased by an earnest apology from Ham? The dichotomy just might be of endless value.

"I'll find you in a moment," Violet told Jack.

He nodded, pressed a kiss to her forehead, and then told Fyfe, "Don't make me regret letting you near her, Fyfe." The implicit threat made Vi grin and Fyfe nod.

"Of course, of course." He held out his hand to Vi who slowly put hers into his. After several silent moments of dancing, where Violet was waiting for him to put words to the implied apology he promised, he scowled at her. "You're going to make me say it, aren't you?"

"Oh yes," Vi agreed brightly. "I'm looking forward to it."

He frowned fiercely.

"Just a hint," Vi's merry voice rang out. "That's not the way to go about it."

Ian Fyfe took in a deep breath, held it, and then said, "You have my deepest regrets for the way I treated you, Lady Wakefield."

"Just Vi," Violet said, grinning at him. "Very pretty. Not so heartfelt, but you hit all the right notes."

"Not heartfelt?" His gaze narrowed on hers and his voice was a bit of a growl when he said, "You ruined everything for me."

"I?" Violet lifted a brow and grinned once again at him. Her mocking glance had him grinding his teeth.

"You set me up."

"I did," Violet agreed. "You took the bait so very well."

Ian Fyfe's fingers dug into her back as he fought his temper.

"If you bruise me," Violet told him merrily, "Jack will contrive for you to be shanghaied. He's neither forgiving nor finished—like my twin—with just tossing you on the street. You were, you know, quite lucky that it was the tired version of Victor you met."

"Yes, well," Ian muttered, "I suppose that pushing past the maid was in poor taste."

"Oh my, yes," Violet agreed. "That was stupid."

"How do I get her to forgive me?" He was trying for supplicating, and given his expression, he actually thought she'd help him out.

"I suggest leaving her be."

The furious expression came back onto his face. "Why is your stupid detective so much better than me?"

"Well, for one," Violet answered plainly, "he'd never have fallen for my trick. For two, he's not stupid. For three, he actually loves her. For four, he's not a total condescending, rude, manipulative, bastard. For five—"

Vi had every intention of continuing until he stormed off the dance grounds, but she'd really been counting on him lasting for longer than a mere four reasons. She followed after to see him shove Oscar Watts and his partner aside and then push past to where Samuel Richards was whispering with Martha.

"That Wakefield shrew is horrible," Fyfe told Martha and Samuel. "She should have been drowned at birth as the devil's progeny. Her husband should beat her daily to change her behavior."

Samuel Richards's gaze was laughing, but what he

said was, "Now Brother Ian, that's no way to speak of one of God's daughters."

Martha snorted and met Vi's gaze. "She *is* a shrew. I have never cared for her myself, but I'll say this for her, I heard what happened—"

Ian Fyfe groaned and muttered, "She set that scenario up!"

"Of course she did, and you fell for it."

"That was hardly fair," he said.

"Chasing someone for their money isn't fair either," Martha told him flatly. "No one made you say what you did to her. She made you upset, and you revealed your true colors."

"Just like you in that...that whore's dress!" Fyfe told her, looking Martha over as though she were a piece of roadside trash.

To Violet's delight, Martha winked at him. "But I'll be going home to a nice house this evening, and tomorrow when I have breakfast, I'll be having it with the woman you say you love. Certainly the woman whose money you love. I wonder what she'll think of this tale."

To Violet's shock, Ian Fyfe slapped Martha hard. She cried out, and Brother Samuel sighed as Fyfe stomped off. "If any man among you seem to be religious, and bridleth not his tongue, but deceiveth his own heart, this man's religion is vain."

Violet shoved Samuel aside and took Martha into her arms. "Shut your mouth."

"She did not make her repentance even one hour." He looked sad as Martha held her cheek, staring at her one-time betrothed.

"Judge not that ye be not judged," Violet snapped.

"You are a blight upon humanity and if you have a truly contrite bone or believing heart, I'd be very much surprised!"

"He didn't even defend me," Martha told Violet. She sounded more infuriated than sad, so Violet just said, "There, there."

Samuel Richards looked between the two women and said gently, "I'll go get your men. I fear that you won't accept my protection when you're so hysterical."

"What protection?" Violet muttered to his back, staring daggers. She should very much like to box his ears.

Martha didn't even look after him. "But he didn't even defend me, Vi. Not at all. He...he...quoted scripture at me."

Violet tried again. "There, there."

"Stop saying that!" Martha hissed. "By Jove, woman! What a disappointment Samuel Richards has turned out to be."

Violet took Martha by the arm and headed towards Jack. As usual, he towered above most of the gents there. His back was towards them, which was good, she thought. She'd hate to see him brought up on charges for beating Ian Fyfe or Samuel Richards.

As they approached Jack and Ham, Martha started prettily weeping. Violet paused a few steps away from their friends and demanded, "Did you...are you play acting?"

"I was struck!"

"A few minutes ago," Violet told her. "Look at your tears! They're slow dribbles. It's very pretty. Do you practice in front of the mirror?"

Martha's gaze narrowed on Vi, but she wailed, "How can you be so cruel?"

Her wail got the attention she wanted, but Victor saw her and immediately stepped behind Lila. Denny looked her over and sighed. "What happened?"

"Ian Fyfe slapped her," Violet announced loudly, to ensure that Rita and Bidlake heard it.

Rita gasped, turning from Bidlake's attention to Vi and Martha. "Why?"

"She was teasing him," Violet told Rita, checking Bidlake's reaction.

"He's hot-tempered," Bidlake told Rita. "Miss Lancaster should have been more careful with her words."

Vi grinned at his reply and winked at Ham before turning to Jack. He examined her. "Did you get slapped too?"

"Not this time," Violet told her husband, grinning at him, "but I suspect that I would not be safe in another round. I don't think he likes us."

"I don't like Martha," Denny agreed. "Not in the least bit."

Martha sniffed and stomped her foot, letting out another pretty tear. "You are supposed to be my friends."

Denny's head tilted at Lila. "Maybe you can explain."

"You have to be nice to other people for them to like you, Martha. This is why you don't have friends from your school days either."

Martha let out another tear and Violet was almost gentle when she asked, "Martha, who are you crying for?"

The girl looked between them, eyes shining, as she

saw Victor carefully not looking at her, and Jack and Ham, who were both passive in their neutrality.

"I have a question," Bidlake asked. "Why do you treat your friends this way? I thought you were singling me out until I saw you teasing Miss Lancaster."

Violet snorted and Rita glanced to the side. Denny slowly answered as though Bidlake was a dullard. "Martha isn't our friend. She's our annoying little sister. Once she stops being annoying, we'll start being much nicer. You'll notice that our meanness also rid her of the fiend Samuel Richards. That man is a conman if ever I saw one. We aren't treating you like a friend either, because you aren't our friend."

"And when Rita accepts my proposal?"

They were all silent as they stared at him. He was, Violet thought, in earnest arrogance. The poor lad. "I wouldn't put all my eggs in that basket, laddie," she told him gently.

"Do you think I'm as easy to get rid of as that fool, Richards?"

Violet looked around the circle of their friends. Even Rita was hiding a smile. Rita's lack of reaction to the assumed engagement was all Violet needed.

To Bidlake, Violet simply said, "Well, yes."

# CHAPTER 7

Martha's mean laugh filled the air, and Ham asked Rita, "I wonder if I might have the next dance."

She looked him over and then put her hand in his. Bidlake gaped as Ham swung Rita into their first dance since she'd left England.

"But I'm a lord."

Violet snorted and told Jack, "Is the beer here as terrible as I suspect?"

He nodded.

"That hotel has a bar that's open late, though, doesn't it? Perhaps we could get some cocktails and then wander the beach at night."

"Yes, please," Lila said. "I did drink some of the beer, and I can't get the taste of it out of my mouth. The flavor has lingered so long, I feel certain that I shall die with it still in my mouth."

They found their way to The Cliff House. It was at

least four floors of hotel rooms and restaurants with a bar that was open late. Violet ordered something with oranges and berries. It was odd, fruity, and had a sprig of mint that somehow tied it all together. She sipped her first slowly and took her second down the steps to the shore.

They danced in the waves with their friends, and she wasn't able to hide her delight at seeing Ham swing Rita into a dance as if they both knew they were meant to be. Violet assumed they hadn't had the conversation that was necessary yet, but they were getting closer. She left them to their romance and let Jack pull her into hers.

When they climbed back up the steps from the shore, they found that the bar was just closing, but Victor persuaded the barman to make them one more round of drinks. The next was sweet with the aftertaste of honey and made Violet miss her sister. She'd had something similar when she'd had her engagement party to that fiend Danvers. Isolde had escaped that mistake, found Tomas, and might have even had her baby by now. Tomas had whisked her away from Lady Eleanor, and the letters were sparse enough that Violet had little doubt he was sending them from post offices that weren't in the town they were actually staying in. From Isolde's last letter to Vi, they intended to return once the baby had been born and Isolde had recovered.

Poor Lady Eleanor, Vi thought, and then set aside her cocktail. If she was having sympathy for her stepmother, she'd had too much to drink. Lady Eleanor adored her children to an obsessive extent, but she'd also driven the wedge between herself and Violet over years of repeated actions.

Violet laid her head against Jack's shoulder as they sat in one of the booths near the window. The sight of the ocean reflecting the moon made Violet sure that she'd never seen anything more beautiful. Perhaps things just as beautiful, but nothing *more* beautiful.

Violet tangled her fingers with Jack and he wrapped his arm around her shoulders. The cool air came in from the windows, and she both enjoyed the fresh scent of the ocean air and was chilled by it without the comfort of his arm.

"I am so glad that we made it through," Violet told Jack. "We could have messed up our lives so easily by letting the little things ruin us before we could realize what was most important."

Jack's answer was a kiss pressed against the top of her head and then another on each of her fingers. Ham and Rita were whispering together, but Violet didn't think they were having *the* conversation. Not the full one. Not with an audience and not at a bar where they'd have to vacate before the conversation could come to its own conclusion.

Vi followed her gaze to Victor who looked as though he'd escaped the weight of the world. He had needed to escape his babies, Vi thought. It was funny how she knew he loved them more than anything except maybe Kate, and yet, he also needed nothing more than to not be breathing the air where they were. If they were fussing, they would be fine, but he wouldn't be able to relax if he heard them crying.

"Do you think we'll be as bad as Kate and Victor?"

"With your imagination? And my experiences? Vi, darling, we'll be so much worse."

Vi winced and then looked back out the window. To her surprise she saw Samuel Richards, Oscar Watts, and Parkington Bidlake conferring at the top of the steps. What were they conspiring over, Vi wondered. Were they making a schedule to throw their favors at Rita's feet? Were they bargaining who had the best chance to scale her defenses? Were they working out a plan to separate her from her friends?

Surely it had to do with Rita, given that they weren't friends outside of that? Perhaps they'd decided to walk their aggression off and ran into each other? If so, Vi hoped they'd continue onto a pub and leave them be at the bar.

"We should go," Violet said, nudging Jack's attention to the gents outside.

"That's an odd trio," Jack murmured. "Makes you wonder what they're up to."

Violet shook her head. It was an odd trio, Jack was right. They were full grown men who'd run into each other at a carnival. Surely that was all it was? They were probably going to drink off their woes. No, Violet thought with a smirk, *Oscar and Bidlake* had been determined to drink their woes, and Samuel Richards had somehow caught them up.

She told Jack her theory, and his shout of laughter pulled everyone's attention. He pointed to the group and told them what he thought.

"He probably is ruining things for them," Martha said, not sounding heartbroken in the least. Her voice was cool and snakelike as her gaze narrowed on him. "Trying to pander for sponsors for his stupid missions. What's so wrong with leaving a couple of gents free to live their lives? Besides, if Bidlake is really a lord I'll eat my hat. And, if Oscar Watts isn't just another friendless third son, I'd be very much surprised. I bet you he was some sort of school boy's ape leader who got let go on their journey for making eyes at the ladies. You have to watch out for the quiet ones, you know. Those spectacles, they proclaim him a man who's pretending to be more serious than he is."

"You don't think they proclaim him a man who has bad vision?"

"I think that they heard Rita was rich and thought it would be easy enough to pursue her. Far more so than when on land where someone else could sneak her away from them. She was trapped on the ship and hadn't even bothered with an escort this time."

"And you were useless," Denny told Martha.

"I am *younger* than Rita, and less experienced. It isn't my fault that she got surrounded."

Lila's head tilted and then she asked slowly, "You were the one who let the rumor out. It wasn't someone hearing Rita's name and thinking oh I wonder if that's Roderick Russell's daughter. Their name isn't that uncommon."

Martha blushed furiously and shook her head, but she'd revealed herself.

"What did you do?" Denny grabbed the back of his neck before stretching it out as though the burden of Martha had already given him knots in his back. "Try to impress someone and set the rumor mill afire? Then you abandoned Rita to all the wolves who showed up to salivate?"

Martha's pretty, slow tear was all the answer they got.

~

"WELL?" Violet demanded as she and Rita left the house with Ham's two puppies, Violet's two small spaniels, and Victor's one spaniel.

"Well," Rita repeated, clucking down at Watson. "They are precious, aren't they?"

"Yes," Vi agreed, and because she was unequivocally on Ham's side, she added, "I did say that I bought them to distract him from you."

"Oh." Rita grinned at Vi. "That is a good one."

"Isn't it?" Vi winked and then clucked at Mary who was nearly worthless on a leash. "It's true though. Did Ham apologize?"

"He told me he was a fool beyond belief, and he'd rather have cut out his tongue than say the things he had said, let alone cause in me the pain that he'd been feeling."

Violet juggled the puppy to clutch her heart. "Oh! That was a good one."

Rita rubbed her head over the top of little Watson's head, accepted a kiss, and then nodded. What she said was, however, "I am pretty sure he practiced it."

"That just means he meant it enough for it to be important."

Rita rolled her eyes. "I am also certain that Parkington Bidlake practiced his honeyed lines yesterday."

Vi groaned. "When it's Bidlake, it's sneaky. When it's Ham, it's lovely."

"Why?" Rita demanded.

She met Rita's blue gaze. Her eyes were tortured, Vi saw, and Violet felt instantly repentant. She put down

Mary, took Watson, and then hugged Rita tightly. "I am sorry."

"Why are you apologizing?"

"I keep pushing Ham at you, and I do love Ham, but Rita—this is about what will make you happy."

Rita's lip quivered. "It would be so easy to get on the next steamship."

Violet had to clench her teeth tight and fiddle with the leashes to keep back her protest.

"My father would be sad, and I wouldn't be happier there than here. I feel like Ham stole my joy in adventuring, and I'm not sure I can give him enough rope to take away the next bit of my joy. I know it's weak Vi, but I don't know if I can do this with Ham again."

"Then don't," Violet told Rita. "Just don't settle for one of those bastards either."

Rita's watery laugh sounded amused enough that Vi breathed a little easier. "I don't know. Oscar is pretty sweet. He was around before the rumors of my money were loosed."

"Of course he was. You're beautiful, clever, kind. You're a catch with or without being your father's only child."

"I am, aren't I?" Rita laughed and then picked up both Mary and Watson. "I've always wanted a dog."

Violet did *not* tell her that Ham would share.

"That is a level of self-control I wasn't sure I could expect."

Vi laughed as she admitted, "I might have bit down so hard in my mouth, it's bleeding a bit."

"Oh baby," Rita said, not sounding sympathetic at all. "Shall we walk down to the pier and then come back?"

Violet followed, huffing a little given that Rita was far stronger. About halfway back, they were both carrying dogs under each arm. The puppies had given up first, followed by Rouge, then Holmes. Victor's Gin was still keeping up, but his tongue was lolling and his breathing was rough.

"We should rest," Violet declared as they passed a café serving tea, scones, and coffee. She dropped into one of the chairs at the outside table and begged water for the dogs along with Turkish coffee, scones, jam, and clotted cream. It was only after she ordered that she asked Rita, "Do you have money?"

Rita stared at Vi long enough that she felt certain she was going to need to chase the girl down and cancel her order, before Rita winked and nodded.

"Minx."

"Shrew."

"Cow."

"Wench."

"Hey now," a deeper voice said, and they turned to the grinning face of Oscar Watts, "that's no way for young ladies to speak to each other."

# CHAPTER 8

*O*nly the ironic twist to Oscar Watt's mouth kept Violet from immediately disliking him. "Hello there. I wonder if I might join you."

Violet nodded before Rita could make excuses. Vi told herself to be nice and lifted Rouge into her lap to give her something to do so she wasn't casting daggered glances at the...the...rogue in front of her.

"You must be Violet," Oscar said with a grin. "Rita described you as angled beauty."

"I do have sharp elbows," Violet agreed.

His shout of laughter made her like him just a little. She had to admit that she liked hearing that he'd listened to Rita well enough to guess her friend's name. They had, of course, been introduced, but Rita would have described Violet in just a way.

"Now Kate is the one who studies the odd subjects like Greek?"

Violet paused and then nodded. "That's our Kate."

"And you and your twin write the V.V. Twinnings novels? Rita told me you based your ingenue, Isla, off of your sister's stupidity."

Violet felt herself being appeased and wondered if she could like this fellow. She didn't want to say yes, but she suspected that she could, in fact, like him rather a lot. "I did."

"That's a cruel blow."

"She deserved it."

"What did she do to you in return?"

Violet's head tilted. "She knew she deserved it."

"So she just took your censure?"

"My censure is very tongue-in-cheek. When it comes to my siblings, it includes well-aimed insults, endless help, and occasional lectures for the good of mankind. You should see my little brother. He's almost human. I'd give him a decade or two, and he'll be tolerable for longer than a few weeks."

Oscar's brows rose from behind his spectacles. He pulled them off and cleaned the lenses with his handkerchief, but Violet's sarcastic smirk was ready when his spectacles were back on his face. "I wonder if she adores you."

"Most do," Violet told him, pressing her lips together to hide her smile.

"Of course they do," he said amiably. "If Rita does, who would not?"

Violet would have replied but the Turkish coffee arrived, and she needed a moment to breathe it in.

"How did you lose all of your fellows?" Oscar asked.

"We snuck out. Like thieves in the night."

Oscar looked to Rita. "I feel sure she's bamming me."

"She is," Rita told him. Violet didn't crow that he seemed so uncertain. The very uncertainty was such a letdown after seeing the sureness of Ham. Vi might not be pushing Rita towards Ham actively anymore, but she was still cheering for him. "We said we're taking the dogs for a walk and then we left."

"Ah," Oscar grinned engagingly. "They probably recognized that you wanted to have a good chitchat and then I intruded."

"You did. Very rudely finagled your way into our gossip."

Oscar smiled sweetly enough, but he blushed at his ears, which unfortunately jutted out just a bit from his spectacle frames.

"Tell me about yourself," Violet ordered as she spread her scone with clotted cream. There was, she told herself, no reason to feel sympathy. He'd need to be able to handle Rita's friends if he was going to...to...finagle his way into their lives.

He accepted the tea Rita poured him. "Well, I graduated from Oxford and had just enough money for a bit of a travel and I thought, why not? I've been gone for years now, really. I took jobs here and there. Did what I could to extend things and always kept enough for a trip home. My father called me back finally and like the obedient son, I have returned."

Violet wasn't sure she quite believed what he said, but she nodded.

"It sounds like the prodigal son, doesn't it?" Rita asked.

Violet nodded instantly. "I think our Oscar is keeping secrets."

"Surely we all have them?" Oscar asked. "This Violet looks like a woman who has buckets and buckets of secrets."

Violet lifted a brow at the idea and didn't object. An objection begged the idea that she was protesting too much. And really, Violet didn't want to know what stories he was imagining up for her; she wanted to know if the stories she was imagining up for him were near the mark.

"What kinds of work did you do?"

"Secretarial work mostly," Oscar said. "A bit of translating. I have a gift for languages which has been quite fortunate. I sold a few articles to English and American papers. Worked for an odd American for quite a while until he married a local woman and whisked her home. That was near Mongolia of all places. Whatever I could do, I did."

If Violet had removed Ham from the Rita equation, she would have imagined up just such a man for Rita. Someone who worked, who was from England and understood her, but someone who wanted to see and know more of the world than their fair isle.

"What is your favorite city?"

"It's an odd answer," Oscar said, "but I quite liked New York City."

"Why?" Violet demanded. She hadn't been yet but she was curious.

"It was just a mixture. You could see so many things and experience so much of the world in such a small place."

"London is diverse," Violet suggested to see what he'd say.

"It is, but it's home. It feels like a city is supposed to feel. New York City is different. That's all. It still feels foreign, but I can eat pasta with Italians and the next night see a parade near Chinatown. Central Park is lovely. I just liked it. In the end, I just liked it."

"Just liking it is a good answer," Violet told him simply. "It is perhaps the perfect answer. Now why do you like Rita?"

"Who else has seen and loved the world as she has?" It was an earnest answer. He grinned Rita, and then turned back at Vi. "She's been on a safari. Ridden elephants. Lived with a monkey. She's eaten the things that would make a traditional English girl blush and gag and she's seen the places I've seen. It's nice to talk to someone who has visited both Montreal and Sri Lanka. When you add in that she's clever and kind? What's not to like?"

"She's shady," Violet told Oscar. "You can't trust her not to break into your hotel room and dig through your things."

"I have nothing to hide," he said, and Violet wasn't quite sure she believed it.

Instead, Violet considered him. "What is your favorite book?"

"That's not a V.V. Twinnings book?"

Violet groaned and saw Rita was hiding a grin. "I am not so easily pandered to."

"Well, one can try."

"You should expect more from Rita's friends."

"I might have made you sound like a pack of zozzled idiots." Rita's evil grin was well-timed and she winked at Violet's lifted brow.

"That's probably a somewhat fair assessment," Violet

admitted. "At least for our most remarkable stories. It's not like you're going to tell about that one time we all stayed in, read novels, and went to bed early after a midmorning nap."

"That does sound pretty nice," Oscar told Violet as though Rita *had* told that tale. It had happened more than once, and really should happen while they were at the seashore. There was something about naps with the ocean waves in the distance.

"We really should adventure again," Violet admitted, "after we nap again. Though I'd prefer not to be sucked into another scheme such as that last one. What shall we do? Choose a way to torture Jack?"

"Shh," Rita hissed and then grinned engagingly at Oscar.

It was, of course, ineffective. Oscar's gaze shot between the two of them and Violet noted his surprise. Rita, it seemed, hadn't explained all her adventures to him. It warmed Violet's heart to realize that Oscar did not know Rita's depths. Had she told him about her mother? Or her aunt? That the aunt had murdered both her mother and stepmother was not something that you led with in friendship, but it was something you shared in love.

Violet looked a question to Rita who shook her head. With great struggle, Violet resisted a cheer. Instead she said, "I believe the dogs have rested sufficiently."

Oscar escorted them on the way back to the house, so Violet let him carry Gin and Holmes while she carried Rouge. The dogs were, without question, spoilt. They almost needed to get a pram if they were going to go on longer walks. Or, Violet amended, they needed to just bring another gent along who *wasn't* Oscar Watts to carry the dogs.

When they reached the house, they left Oscar at the sidewalk without the least bit of concern.

"Riding this morning?" Rita asked.

"Jack told the servants to go over and reserve us horses for this morning."

Violet waited just outside the door with Rita, who finally said, "Don't say it."

Violet said it. "If you can't tell him about your mother and your aunt, he's not the man for you."

Rita's withering glare was enough for Violet to hold up her hands.

"I'm sorry."

"You are not. You're pointing out his flaws, and it's not like I want to tell *anyone* that my aunt murdered my mother and stepmother. No one wants to tell that story or even to know that it is their past. I like to pretend that I'm not the idiot who loved and traveled with the very woman who stole my mother from me."

Violet shot Rita a quelling look. It wasn't as if Violet didn't understand. Her cousin—whom she had been raised with as a near sister—had murdered their great-aunt. Given that Aunt Agatha had stood in the place of Violet's own dead mother, Vi understood. It was a burden that was suffocating at times. The truth hit you, and the days turned grey. The things that people would do to those they *loved* for money or another love. It was enough to send one to their beds for life. But, Violet reminded herself, she focused on the good. She focused on the kind, and she focused on love.

"I would have said that to you regardless of Ham. To my dismay, I like Oscar."

Rita examined Violet's face carefully and begrudgingly, and Violet repeated, "I like Oscar."

"I do too."

They stared at each other. A silent argument, so they didn't ruin their reunion. Violet was thinking *very* loudly that Oscar might be all right, but he *still* wasn't the right man for Rita if she couldn't trust him with what happened in her family. Rita was silently telling Violet that just because she hadn't *yet* said it didn't mean she never could.

"It's early days yet," Violet admitted.

"I'm all of a jumble inside. There's a part of me that feels like I've promised Ham my heart and my hand because I've come back after your letter and his—"

A throat cleared and they both gasped and turned back to the sidewalk where Ham and Jack stood at the bottom of the steps. They had clearly heard at least the last of what Rita had said.

Both Violet and Rita stared at Ham, and Violet was cursing like a sailor inside of her head because he'd overheard Rita's confession. Given Rita's deep blush, her friend was doing the same.

"How about," Ham offered, "I tell you here that I don't expect that from you. All I ask is a fresh chance." Before Rita could answer, Ham carefully added, "Whatever your answer now, later, or never, I consider you one of my dearest friends, and I want that to continue regardless of the rest."

"Can you do that?" Rita's question was a doubtful wail.

Ham hesitated and then he said, "Rather than lose you entirely? I could do anything."

Violet opened the front door and brought the dogs inside. Jack closed the door behind them, leaving Rita and Ham outside. "Well."

"Well," she repeated. She winked at him and then stuck her ear to the door.

"Vi!"

She turned, making a face. "It's too thick to hear through. I remember what that feels like, so I suppose I should accept that I shouldn't be listening."

Jack's eyes glinted with humor and his telling glance to the door she *couldn't* hear through was pointed. But he only said, "Were we so bad?"

"We were close."

Violet let go of the leashes and jumped into his arms, wrapping her own around his neck. "I am so glad we're on this side of things."

The breath-stealing kiss he gave her was all the answer she got.

"Surely you have a bedroom," Martha said from the stairs in disgust. "Wait until I write to my mother. She'll be appalled."

"Oh my goodness," Violet groaned into Jack's neck where she was hiding her blush. "If we keep tripping over each other at the worst possible moment, someone is sure to break something."

"I vote we start with her."

They both looked at Martha who held up her hands and muttered, "I just wanted to eat. But who can eat after that? A virtuous woman. I hardly think so."

Violet bit down on her bottom lip to hold back the

shout of laughter. Her laughter couldn't be stopped, so she muffled it against Jack's chest, finally muttering, "She's ruining all my fun."

"Mine too," Jack said to the top of Violet's head as he dropped a kiss in her hair.

"I meant with my joke," Violet said catching *something* in his tone.

"I didn't," Jack told her.

She smacked his arm and started up the stairs calling, "I'm going to hold a baby or two."

"We're leaving in an hour to go riding, Vi. Don't forget to change."

"Not nearly enough time to change and snuggle," she called back, "but I shall endeavor to persevere."

# CHAPTER 9

*T*he stable willing to let them take a horse for the morning had enough for them all, but both Martha and Denny ended up with ancient beasts while Jack and Ham had near-wild monsters.

Violet laughed at all four of them as they led the horses away from the stable. Only Lila had refused to go riding, but the disgusted look she'd given Denny had said it was his worries for the baby that was holding her back.

"How do you feel?" Vi asked Kate.

"I feel like a cold and cruel mother who abandoned her children on the garbage heap."

Violet snorted as she amended, "I believe you mean with *two* well-qualified, well-researched, well-respected nannies who will probably watch them sleep and be paid top dollar to do so."

"Or that," Kate muttered ungraciously. She pulled on her sleeves and rubbed the back of her neck as though she didn't know what to do with her hands when she wasn't holding a baby. Vi didn't disguise her grin when she saw Kate's subtle, baby-soothing sway. It seemed she didn't have her not-holding-a-baby legs.

"Or that," Rita repeated. She followed Vi's gaze to the swaying Kate and grinned as widely at Vi.

They were all wearing riding garb. Kate was in a classic black jacket, black riding pants, and black riding boots. She looked amazing even though her jacket was open and her pants were a bit snugger than usual. She had *nearly* recovered her pre-baby form.

Violet, on the other hand, had selected a deep purple jacket and black pants when she'd acquired her riding gear. She'd done it with about as much subtle irony as a sledgehammer. Especially when she'd had her sleeves embroidered with ivy and she wore a grey shirt underneath complete with violets on each collar.

Rita's jacket was blue sapphire with quite a lovely large button at her narrow waist. The fabric had probably been purchased to draw attention to her large blue eyes. However, after what had clearly been a good cry, it drew attention to the redness in her eyes, the puffy dark circles underneath, and set off her general paleness. She probably should have napped the late morning away with Lila, but something had her refusing to stay behind.

She was putting on a good show. Without the crying evidence, Violet would have assumed that Rita was as fine as usual. The rest of them were pretending that Rita hadn't wept after her talk with Ham, except for poor Ham who had a clench to his jaw that said he was about one breath from thrusting his fist through a wall.

"I've never gone riding on the shore," Kate muttered.

"It would be nice to not feel like such a monster while doing it. Why do I feel bad for leaving the babies?"

"Darling Kate," Victor said, "Breathe in slowly, let it out slowly. Think of the girls in a wonderland of clouds and fairies. That was how I got through last night."

"That and cocktails," Kate muttered.

"Cocktails did help. Shall we stop and have some?"

"No! Let's go riding. I can have fun still."

Violet grinned at the two of them. Victor had never lost that half-besotted, half-shocked by his good fortune look as he gazed at her with love. He grinned, kissed her soundly, and lifted her onto her horse.

She scowled down at him, but he just winked and rubbed her thigh before mounting his own horse.

"You know what you're missing to truly enjoy yourself?" Violet asked Kate.

"What?" Her scowl told Violet that Kate expected a sarcastic answer.

"Some sort of treatise."

"Oh good idea," Victor said. He adjusted the leather satchel he was carrying. "It turns out that I have champagne, a blanket for the sand, and a treatise on *The Sea Creatures of the Caribbean*. What do you say, Kate? We'll learn about these creatures and then take the girls to meet them. I can just see them dabbling their toes in perfectly blue water, can't you?"

Kate frowned at Victor, but Violet had little doubt Kate was intrigued. She'd lost the look of carrying a mountain of guilt and her head cocked as she imagined it.

"I bet they have rum there," Violet added. "I bet he only wants to go because of the rum."

"We *are* running low from our trip to Cuba and my friend, Javier, has proven to be unreliable. I have sent him money four times, and he's never sent me a bottle."

"Darling," Kate said, patting his cheek from the back of her horse, "that's because he is stealing from you."

Victor had to know it was true, but hearing it said aloud seemed to deflate his happiness. It took Kate a few minutes of murmured promises about the Caribbean, blue seas, dipping the twins' toes in the water, and the general happiness it would give her to study something new for Victor to have his cheery outlook again.

"How much of that was an act?" Rita asked Vi.

"Oh, all of it." Vi patted the neck of her dappled mare. "I am ready to fly on this lady. How about you?"

"I believe if we don't take off immediately," Ham said, "Jack and I might be thrown and trampled."

With a whoop, Denny heeled his horse. She turned back to him and seemed to scowl before taking one slow step forward. Rita choked on her laugh but Violet didn't bother to hold hers back. She circled Denny as Jack and Ham rode ahead.

"Come along, lovey," she called to Denny, letting her horse hurry ahead before she guided her back to circle Denny again.

Denny attempted another jolly whoop in attempt to energize his horse. It didn't work. Violet was crying she was laughing so hard. Kate and Victor had looked back at Denny and left him behind without an ounce of regret.

"This isn't fair," Denny said, but he noted Rita's grin and the fading of her whiteness and tried another jolly whoop.

"Maybe if you get off and push her along?" Rita called.

"Oh," Denny groaned. He pushed up on his stirrups to see Jack and Ham, who had gone far ahead with their wilder mounts. The pier was barely a half-kilometer from where they were, and Jack and Ham would be there long before the rest of them made it.

Denny tried again. Martha's horse was just behind Denny's, and if anything Martha's mount made Denny's look speedy. Martha, however, yawned, shaded her gaze, and then half-closed her eyes as though a nap version of a morning ride was just what she needed.

Unlike Rita, Martha seemed unaffected by the day previous. Her gaze was clear, even with a bit of swelling on her face from where she was slapped.

Violet felt that the rest of her friends might be *more* bothered by the slap than Martha herself was. In fact, Violet thought that they might be even more bothered by the fact that Martha seemed to think that being slapped by a man of her acquaintance didn't need to cause more of a reaction than fake tears.

The ride would have been agonizing if Denny didn't embrace the absurdity of his mount. Eventually Rita and Violet raced each other around Denny until he called, "Oh-ho."

Jack had raced back towards them. The furious gallop was different than when he'd been letting his horse have its head.

Violet pulled up, knowing without question that something was wrong. She looked beyond Jack to see Ham had dismounted. Perhaps he'd fallen? But, no. He was dismounted, but he was bending over an object in the water. Ignoring the lap of the waves against his boots wasn't something he'd do as easily as the rest of them.

One part of Violet's mind told her to buy him new boots for some random holiday. The other noted the heap that Ham was looking at. Black mound. Was it garbage? But no, even from the distance and without seeing clearly, she knew what it was.

Jack's intent expression had told her, she just hadn't wanted to believe it. Jack wouldn't have left Ham if he were hurt. Jack wouldn't come racing back towards them for a mound of garbage. If he was bothered, he'd just have someone clean it up. Then when you added in Ham letting his boots be ruined?

There was a body in the water being lapped by the waves near the pier.

Denny's horse slowed as it reached her, then stopped. His comic whooping had come to an end, and his gaze was fixed upon Ham.

Denny glanced sideways at Vi. He had lost the humor in his gaze too. "Do you see what I see?"

"What is taking so long?" Martha snapped. "If you stop for every random shell, these old things will never live long enough to get back, and I don't want to walk in my riding boots. They pinch."

Neither of them answered. Rita had raced towards Kate and Victor who had taken a wider path, but when she noticed that Denny and Vi stopped, she circled back to them. When she arrived, she took in their expressions and followed their gazes to the intently approaching Jack and Ham in the distance. Ham's horse had been let loose and started slowly walking back towards his stable without a reaction from Ham.

Rita's gaze widened. "No."

"I think so," Violet said.

"You think what?" Martha demanded. "My goodness, do we go or go back? Sitting here isn't fun."

"Be quiet," Denny ordered with unaccustomed seriousness.

"Why are you always so mean?"

Denny looked at Violet. "She needs to go home now. Her mother will never forgive Lila and me."

"You have a baby coming," Rita told him comfortingly. "Until Martha can say the same, you'll slide past this one."

"This what? Mama will believe Lila over me when it comes to my engagement. I think we should just all forget it."

"Oh, she's dim," Denny told Rita. "I forget between visits."

"She's not dim," Rita told Denny. "She's just so self-absorbed that she doesn't see anything that doesn't affect her."

Denny shrugged as though it were the same. Jack was nearly back to them, and Violet had gone from sure to convinced. She felt the darkness pressing, and she tried to focus on the good.

Vi closed her eyes and muttered to herself. "Rita is back. Ham and Jack will do what needs to be done. Vivi and Agatha are in the world. Puppy breath. Warm chocolate."

"I brought the ingredients for that chocolate cocktail," Denny told her gently. "And I have ginger wine too. I might have also smuggled a few boxes of chocolates."

"Why are we suddenly babying Vi?" Martha asked with a scowl.

"She doesn't respond well to dead bodies. Her soul isn't as cold as mine."

Martha gaped.

Violet pressed her fingers to her forehead. "It could have been an accident. Maybe some drunk went walking on the pier and slipped in."

Jack finally reached them. His gaze was already fixed on Vi. "We need to head back and get a doctor as quickly as possible."

"What's happening?" Rita asked. She was staring at Ham, who had pulled the body from the water.

Jack's gaze was steady on Vi, full of love and concern, as he carefully said, "There's been a murder."

# CHAPTER 10

"Surely it could be an accident." Violet knew she was begging, but she really needed it to be an accident.

The chances of an accident when Jack had declared it a murder were highly unlikely. He didn't want her to deal with the effects of a murder any more than she did. Possibly more given how he was inclined to protect her.

Jack shook his head.

"Was he shot?"

Jack shook his head.

"Knife in the back?" Denny asked. He was sliding back into his lazy humor, but it seemed his somewhat disgusting joke was in fact a very good guess.

Violet groaned, imagining it already.

"Who is the dead guy?" Martha sounded bored and she had already turned her horse back to the stable.

Jack paused. "It's Samuel Richards."

Violet's mouth dropped open but Martha screamed

dramatically sending her lazy horse trotting sideways and tossing her head.

"Bloody hell." Denny's disgusted look towards Martha summed up all of their reactions. It was bad enough that someone they knew had died, but Martha—who had pretended to love him—was going to beat this dead horse. "I'll go for the constables."

Denny actually got off his horse, handed Vi the reins, and started to jog towards the stable, but Rita said, "Take my horse."

By the time Denny had taken off and Jack had returned to Ham, Victor and Kate had joined them. "What's happening?"

Martha wailed in reply. Violet looked at Rita and jerked her head towards Martha. Rita shook hers in refusal. Victor groaned and lifted Martha down, but Kate had dismounted as well and he shoved Martha at Kate.

It wasn't who Martha wanted, and she cast her tear-filled eyes towards Victor, who backed up. Violet wanted to smirk as Martha stomped her foot, but she was still reeling.

They must have had a telephone at the stables because in the minutes since they'd been watching from a distance, Jack had made it back to Ham, and the autos were beginning to arrive.

They had all dismounted to watch, and when Denny returned, he joined in the distant viewing of the crime scene. The last thing Vi wanted was a closer look to add her to personal album of horrible things. Instead she focused on the official-looking types with uniforms and a stretcher. They were approaching Ham. Vi and Rita stood side-by-side as they watched Ham shake the fellows' hands.

"He must be telling them who he is," Rita murmured. "He's going to get pulled into this case."

"The local boys would be stupid to not use Jack and Ham. They discovered the body, they're Yard men. These fellows can't have the same experience." Victor's reasoning was sound and unnecessary. Violet and Rita would have said the same thing.

"Maybe they won't ask for help," Rita said quietly.

She knew it wasn't likely, so did Violet. But Vi didn't want to get involved in another case. She was still dealing with the nightmares from the last one. They all centered on Kate giving birth in prison and no one helping the babies.

Violet pressed her face into Rita's shoulder. "Kate's not in prison."

Kate looked down at Violet and then patted her head. "I'm not. I'm not going either, love."

"I'd break you out and rescue the babies."

Victor groaned. "Is that what you're dreaming about now? Didn't your friends say that the aunt was going to take that woman's baby?"

Violet nodded. It didn't matter that the baby that spurred Violet's dreams was going to be all right, her sleeping mind didn't care about that. Her sleeping mind tortured her regardless of the realities.

Violet took in a deep breath and slowly let it out.

"You need to write a story where that baby is somehow benefited by what happened."

Violet's scoffing look was enough for Victor to grab Vi, hug her tightly, and say, "Kate is fine. The twins are fine. I'm fine. Jack is fine. You are not fine. Stretch your mind, Vi. Write the story, give the money to a new charity you make for prison babies. Somehow make it better if you can."

Violet shoved Victor even if he was probably right. "Well, I suppose we could interfere again."

"Yes," Denny said. "Can we have the chalkboards back?"

"I was trying to pretend my life wouldn't be like that anymore."

"Vi, darling," Denny said in a gentle voice, "that last round with Jovie and too much alcohol only worked because Pammy was drunk and actually loved her baby. If she was one of those infanticide women, it never would have happened." Violet sighed and Denny grinned in victory. "Yes! The chalkboards are back."

"This is where you contain your enthusiasm so you aren't the next victim," Rita advised dryly.

Denny buttoned his mouth shut and Martha tried wailing again to get their attention. Denny told her dryly, "You should be careful, love. You have to be Ham's first suspect."

"But I was already a murder suspect," Martha whined as though that somehow prevented her from being one again.

Denny looked at Violet as if to ask if she'd heard what he'd heard. "That doesn't exclude you now," he told the girl.

"But we weren't even engaged anymore," Martha snapped. Her tears had stopped and Violet took a moment to admire the acting that had created such believable, and yet still pretty, tears.

"You were engaged, however, and you threw him over." Denny's mouth was twitching.

Martha stomped her foot. "He threw me over!"

"He seemed to want to make amends when we met him at the carnival."

Martha crossed her arms over her chest and hissed, "He wanted me to talk to Rita and Vi about giving him money. He'd begged me to talk to Rita the whole steamship voyage. He'd have been pursuing her too if he'd thought—for a second—she'd give him a chance."

Rita shook her head and looked towards where the body was being loaded onto the stretcher. Even from this distance, they could see his arm drop from under the blanket and dangle lifelessly.

"Oh," Violet said, turning away. She should have turned away long before. "Bloody hell."

"Let's go home," Rita said. "Our being here will just distract Jack and Ham."

Victor nodded, and they turned towards the stable, walking the horses back. Jack and Ham's horses had passed them long ago and had already been stabled by the time they'd returned.

"At least they are well trained enough to go home," Violet said when they passed Jack's horse.

"They just know where their food comes from."

They left the stables and walked towards the house. Denny disappeared on the way, and Vi had little doubt that their parlor would be full of chalkboards. Before that happened, she wanted to attempt a nap.

She climbed the steps to her bedroom and knocked on Lila's door.

"Yes?"

Violet pulled off her boots the moment she reached Lila's room and then lay down on the end of Lila's bed. A moment later, Rita joined them.

"You look terrible," Lila told Rita.

"Thank you," Rita told Lila. "You might be glowing."

"It's the baby."

"Have you decided upon a name?"

Lila shook her head. "Denny only likes names that are also funny, and I'm not doing that to our daughter."

"Denny is currently getting chalkboards."

Lila groaned.

"He's very excited."

"I am sure he is."

"It's Samuel Richards," Rita told Lila and watched her drop her face into her hands. "The dead man."

"Martha is going to be intolerable."

"Denny told her she's the main suspect. He's an evil genius since it took her from wailing to insisting upon all the reasons she's innocent."

Lila shook her head. "My mother will never forgive me."

Violet lay back on the bed, dropped her arm over her eyes, and muttered, "We are cursed. You'll have to explain to your mother that we didn't mean to offend whichever god has laid this on us, and that if we could only find out who, we'd find a way to make things right."

Rita laughed and then took the space next to Violet. "You know, to the local boys we'll be suspects."

"And all your lovers," Lila said. "They had to have known Richards from the steamship. It'll be fun to watch Ham question them and see who whines to you."

Rita did not look nearly as amused at the prospect.

"At least it'll divide the whiners from the rest of the pack."

"There is no pack," Rita said flatly. "There is either Ham or none of them."

"But there will always be us," Lila said, patting Rita's hand. "From a person who waited longer than I wanted to marry, there really is no reason to rush. You can give yourself and Ham time to figure out what you want and make sure you fit."

"First," Rita groaned, "let's find the killer and get rid of these fortune hunters."

"Then you can slowly torture Ham until you've deemed it enough for turning your love aside."

"He didn't," Rita admitted.

Vi lifted her arm, staring and Rita dropped her own arm over her face.

"He told me he loved me more than he thought was possible. He said I made him believe in fairytale love. He told me he wanted me more than he wanted his next breath."

"Oh lovely," Lila said, tearing up and then scowling as she had to smudge away the tear before it ruined her kohl liner.

"Then he said he was too old for me, too poor for me, too set in his ways for me, and he'd never, ever be good enough for me."

Violet rolled her eyes. Boys were so dumb in their misplaced chivalry.

"Oh!" Lila groaned.

"Lila!" Martha shouted from the hall and then burst into the room. Her kohl liner was smeared, but Violet's head cocked.

"You didn't have kohl on before."

Martha glared at Violet, and then she twisted her face in horror and went to throw herself on Lila's shoulder, but Lila held up a quick hand. "I might sick up."

Violet noticed the lie in Lila's gaze.

Martha dropped to her knees next to where Lila had been napping and took her sister's hand. "Lila, it's the most devastating news!"

"The man who decided to exchange his love for you for money has died, and you're a suspect in his murder?" Lila said blandly.

"No! Why would I be? Who could think that I would kill anyone?"

Lila's mouth pursed. "Well, perhaps anyone who knew you at eleven years old? As I recall, you cut off one of my braids."

"Mother let you bob your hair after, so you should have thanked me."

Lila's narrowed gaze was not enough to quell her sister.

"I'm going to tell Mother." Martha fell back on her same old threat.

"You know," Rita said musingly. "Kate made an interesting point about how having a baby on the way will pull Lila ahead of you. You aren't going to be able to blame everything on her anymore. Perhaps your mother will even point out how you should be helping her instead of blaming Lila every time you dig yourself a hole and jump in."

"She won't!"

"She will," Rita told Martha in a way that declared it

an utter certainty. For the first time that day, Martha paled.

"She won't." It was not convinced. It could even have been described as tremulous.

"She will, and she'll be extra furious with you. Now your choices are your own fault *and* you made things harder on your sister."

Martha shook her head, but she was pale. Far paler, it seemed, than being a murder suspect caused. Far more upset than when Samuel Richards had chosen missionary money over her.

"In fact," Rita mused, "I think I'll be writing to her myself about what I witnessed on the steamship. Lila can send it with her own letter updating her mother on how she feels."

"Lila never writes to Mama!"

"Lila is too smart to miss this advantage."

The noise Martha made next could only be described as a squawk.

"Unless," Violet said slowly. She glanced between Lila and Rita and then back at Martha.

"Unless?" Martha looked wretched and hopeful at the same time.

"I suppose I could be persuaded to keep my thoughts to myself," Rita started. "Not tell your mother of your, shall we call them, indiscretions?"

"I don't think we should," Martha said. "Light-heart foibles."

"Regardless," Rita said, lifting a brow. "You'll need to answer each and every question that Violet, Jack, and Ham put to you regarding Richards."

Martha nodded frantically.

"*Without,*" Rita sat up and directly met Martha's gaze, "and I cannot make this clear enough—*theatrics.*"

Lila snorted and Martha shot her a nasty look.

"With respect towards the rest of us," Rita added.

"She won't be able to do that," Lila said.

"Then her mother will hear about Mr. Benedict Stover."

Martha shook her head frantically.

"We'll start when Denny gets back," Violet told Martha. "Go away. Lila is resting."

Martha frowned and then snapped her mouth shut, stomping from the room. She bypassed Kate in the hallway where she walking one of the twins and patting her back.

# CHAPTER 11

"Kate!"

She came into the room and handed Violet baby Agatha. "Let me just get Vivi."

A few moments later and Vivi joined Agatha on the bed, kicking her legs. Both of them were bright-eyed and curious as Kate looked down on them.

"How was it when we got back?" Rita asked carefully.

"I crept up the stairs like a thief in the night, put my ear to the doorway, and found Poppy rocking Agatha's cradle while Jane was singing to Vivi."

"So they were fine?"

Kate frowned fiercely at all of them, but no one was teasing her. "They were fine. Completely happy. I felt let down." Violet's head cocked and Kate continued. "I wanted them to have wanted me and been unhappy without me. I wanted them to wail in relief at my presence and then make that little trembly lip that says they're sad but all is well when Mama is here. I might have cried and then told Victor I had gone mad and sent him out for ice cream, chocolate, and fish and chips."

Violet bit down on her bottom lip and fiddled with her wedding ring in a failed attempt to not laugh at Kate.

"Shut up," Kate moaned and then placed a hand on Vivi's head as Violet placed Agatha on her lap.

"They love you more than anything," Violet told Kate carefully.

"They stop crying for Victor more than me."

"Did you want us to hold your hand and agree that all is very hard because your beautiful, healthy babies are happy?" Lila asked dryly.

"Wait until it's you," Kate said meanly. "You think you won't go mad, know you've gone completely crazed, and won't be able to stop yourself? Because it'll be you too."

Lila's expression said that it would never be her.

"Oh what do you know? Look at your ankles! They're beautiful. Have you sicked up even once?"

"Twice." Lila's evil grin made Kate throw a pillow at her. Rita and Violet were carefully saying nothing.

"Wise," Kate said to them, tucking her hair behind her ear. "I—"

Rita patted Kate's leg before she apologized again. "Ham said he wanted to have children right away."

The silence immediately shifted to a tenseness with everyone holding their breath and not wanting to say the wrong thing.

"I want to marry him and have babies right away."

Violet put her hand over her mouth to hold back all of the things she needed to say about that.

"But, I don't know if I can trust him that far. I don't know if he won't shift on me again."

Violet was nodding behind her hands, holding everything in.

"I'm angry," Rita said blankly. "I'm so angry it's boiling up in me and I don't know how to get past it. I threw my heart at his feet and he acted like he was doing me a favor by telling me no."

Violet dropped her hands. It wasn't like she didn't see how that would break everything down.

"I don't want to spend the rest of my life remembering how that felt, and I don't know if I can forget, so instead, I'm just holding my breath to see if things change."

"That's wise," Kate told Rita. "Anger and hurt is no foundation for a marriage. Forgiveness, however, is."

"So wait until I decide if I can truly forgive him?"

Lila nodded. "While we're throwing out wisdom, no one is going to make you angrier or more hurt than Hamilton Barnes if you marry him. It isn't all sweetness, kisses, and love. There's a lot more feelings to marriage than that."

"I have wanted to murder Victor at least two dozen times." Kate let her finger trail over Vivi's brow. "I was about one blunt instrument and scream of rage from doing it when he let our last nanny go."

Denny threw open the door and demanded, "Did you hear?" He paused in the doorway. "I can see you did. It's very tense in here. Did I do something wrong or is this about Ham?"

"It's not about you, laddie. That's all you need to know." Lila held out her hand and Denny pulled her up and then scooped up Vivi. "Hello, my little princess. Hello, darling. May I use you for a shield, sweet angel?

These ladies are scary right now. The first thing you need to know is that you're a dangerous creature too."

Lila rolled her eyes, but she had a gentle smile.

"The chalkboards have arrived. I bribed them to a ridiculous extent, but they aren't the pretty matching things of your London house, Vi."

Violet rose and followed Denny down to the parlor. The house they'd taken for the week was quite a massive thing with a parlor that left the one in her London house almost too small. The fireplace was at the far corner with two couches and several chairs in front of it. There was a second seating area farther down the room which was too long to comfortably talk with someone near the fireplace to the door. It ran the full length of the large house which had taken all of Violet's party without a problem.

Martha was sitting with her arms folded, pouting. She scowled at Violet, who glanced around the room with the baby in arms.

"Line them up against that wall," Violet told the servants. "Move the furniture, and then line the sofas so that there are two layers of seating while we examine this situation."

"Ma'am?" The housekeeper had nodded to the maid and two young men who worked in the house to start moving the furniture. "What situation, may I ask?"

"There's been a—"

"Murder!" Martha finished, too excited for anyone's comfort. She let a slow tear drop. "My—my—betrothed."

"Oh! You poor dear!" Mrs. Levitt took the prettily weeping Martha into her arms, and Violet didn't bother pointing out that Martha was breaking the agreement for theatrics. Rita could police that while Violet turned her attention to the details of this madness.

She took the new box of chalk and one of the half-dozen chalk holders that Denny had purchased and put it together. The maid had scrubbed down what looked like a pub menu from the first board, and Violet wrote down the names:

SAMUEL RICHARDS—
MARTHA LANCASTER—
PARKINGTON BIDLAKE—
IAN FYFE—
OSCAR WATTS—
VERNON ATKINSON—
THOSE TWO BIG BLOKES FROM THE FAIR—

Vi's mouth twisted as she added on a separate board:

DENNY LANCASTER—
LILA LANCASTER—
VIOLET WAKEFIELD—
JACK WAKEFIELD—
RITA RUSSELL—
HAMILTON BARNES—
VICTOR CARLYLE—
KATE CARLYLE—

The maid was staring at Violet in utter horror. Vi grinned and winked. "Don't worry, dear. We didn't kill him, but it's always best to be able to tell the constables why it wasn't you when you had a bit of a reason."

The maid's expression looked no less horrified. "But why would you have a reason?"

"Oh we all hated him," Violet said casually. "If I were a colder creature, I would say he wasn't much of an addition to the human race, but I am trying not to be a heartless wretch."

Martha sniffled, but she was careful to make sure her voice carried when she spoke. "You aren't doing a very good job of it."

"We haven't thrown you onto the street yet, have we?"

Violet turned from Martha and looked at the worried maid. "Maybe you could have Cook send in a rather large selection of sandwiches and tea things?"

The maid rushed from the parlor as though the hounds of hell were chasing her just as there was a knock at the front door. Vi glanced towards the door, at Martha who lifted a lazy brow and shook her head, and then went to answer it herself with Agatha still settled in the crook of Vi's arm.

There was a constable on the steps. He was young, tall, handsome, with large blue eyes, a baby face, and a uniform that bulged with rather a lot of muscles.

"Hello," Violet said, trying to hide her smile at his earnest expression.

"I've been sent to Mrs. Wakefield by Mr. Barnes and Mr. Wakefield." He looked down at his feet and Violet noticed the trunk along with two suitcases. "They've assigned me the job of working through this paperwork and said I might find a willing secretary here."

Vi rolled her eyes and stepped back, gesturing towards the double parlor. She followed him in closely to see Martha take him in and then sit up quickly. She went from lazy to lounging goddess in one swift shift.

"This is the destroyed betrothed." Vi's dry tone was lost on the constable who nodded and then crossed to her, holding out his hand.

"Martha Lancaster." She held hers out palm-down, but he didn't take the bait to kiss it.

"My deepest condolences."

"This is the constable that Jack has sent," Violet told Martha. "I didn't catch your name."

He blushed furiously as he hadn't given it. "Constable Henry, ma'am."

Violet smiled at him. "We'll get to that stuff. We're waiting for everyone else to come down."

The constable stared, only realizing in the coming moment that she had already taken over. Instead of objecting, he slid into the role of her helper naturally.

"Separate what you've found in there, will you? I supposed Jack and Ham already looked it over?"

"They said he was a rather odd fellow with all these things." Constable Henry was already spreading the contents out on a table.

Violet glanced them over and then opened one to look it over more carefully. "If I had to guess, I would say this is a ledger of shipments not scriptures."

"That is what Detective Inspector Wakefield said. He also said that you might be able to make heads or tails of it."

There wasn't even the slightest trace of doubt on Henry's face, and Violet liked him all the better for it. For once the rarity of her having something to contribute and being female wasn't causing every passing male a loud moment of disbelief.

Denny was the first to arrive with Vivi still in his arms. He was followed rather more slowly by Lila, who swanned into the room, noted her sister's obsession with the constable and groaned. Rita, Kate, and Victor were next, followed by the maid.

"Officially, Henry is going through these things," Violet announced, gesturing to the tables they'd put together with Richards's papers as she shifted Agatha. "Unofficially, we'll be riffling through it, discovering why someone would want to kill him—other than us of course—and seeing if we can't help Jack and Ham narrow down the suspects while they do the boring stuff."

Constable Henry had laughed awkwardly at the comment about their being suspects, but no one else had. He stared at them as if they were snakes and then raised his hand.

"Yes, Constable?" Violet asked.

"Mrs. Wakefield, why are you suspects?"

"We hated him," Denny told the constable gleefully.

"Rabidly," Rita added.

"I didn't—" Martha started, but Rita snapped, "Careful."

Martha's tears stopped in the next second.

Violet crossed to Rita and put Agatha in her arms, hoping that holding the angel would soften her towards having a baby with Ham and putting him out of his misery as well.

She went to the chalkboard to their names and started making notes. It was important, she thought, to move through all those who had motives even if she knew they weren't killers. In ruling them out and pondering on the nature of the man, she found it easier to add comments and questions to other names. Just because Martha hated Samuel for throwing her over didn't mean she was the *only* woman he used for his missionary work.

"Did anyone *see* him doing missionary work? Or doing more than quoting scripture and calling everyone brother and sister?"

Rita looked baffled. "Who would pretend to be a man of the cloth?"

"A criminal," Lila answered lazily. "It *would* be just like Martha to fall for a man because he was religious and discover later he was just another liar and cheat."

"I say," Constable Henry said, "I mean...well...that's rather a bit much, isn't it?"

Violet smiled at the innocent lamb and was gentle as she told him, "I believe you'll find that most people who are murdered are either wives, daughters, or sisters hurt by the men who are supposed to love them or men who have given rather a lot of people reason to kill them."

She turned to the board. "Look at us. We all rather hated him a lot. Since he was trying to romance Martha to get at our money, we have a compelling motive from the outside."

"And from the inside?"

Vi's grin was wicked, but Denny beat her to the answer. "Oh, we'd have let Martha marry the fellow and suffer. For it to be one of us, we'd have to be willing to murder to save Martha from him. We all disliked him, certainly, but I think that might have been true of nearly everyone who knew him."

"That's not true," Martha said. "I saw him laughing with Lord Bidlake. I saw him playing poker with Oscar and Ian. I saw him smoking with Vernon and several of the mates on the steamship. I saw him telling jokes with a few of the deckhands. He might have been a bit...a bit... much with *you* but that was probably because you were horrible from the start!" She looked as though she'd won an argument and Violet went to the teacart before she boxed Martha's ears.

Kate handed over a Turkish coffee and murmured, "Interesting move putting the baby in Rita's arms."

"Interesting move bringing them in here."

The sisters-in-law grinned at each other. Vi sipped her coffee, set it down, and then said, "Have some, Henry. You'll need it to deal with us."

"You will," Martha said sourly, but the constable grinned as he poured himself a cup of black tea and took a butter biscuit.

# CHAPTER 12

"Do we know when he was stabbed?"

"Sometime after 2:00 a.m.," Constable Henry replied. "They only know that because it was when you saw him. If the doctor was able to find out more, I haven't heard yet."

Violet's mouth twisted. "Rita, write out notes to invite Bidlake and Oscar Watts to dinner tomorrow. They must be at The Cliff House, right?"

Rita groaned, but she rose, giving the baby to Lila and crossing to the writing desk.

"Perfume them," Lila called. "Do you have the scent of ready money? If you don't, Violet might."

"Shut it," Violet and Rita said in unison. Violet amended with, "A little perfume might not be a bad idea."

"Shut it," Rita grumbled, but she frowned at Denny, who was pacing with Agatha, and nodded, and he rang for a maid to send for it.

Violet took a few minutes to sort the papers as

quickly as she could and then sighed. "Constable, you sort these to what looks like ledgers and letters, and for anything else, ask us."

He nodded.

There was a map in the pile that covered many of the places that Rita and Martha had journeyed, with X's on certain locations.

"Kate, darling, you're the cleverest of us. Would you see if you can put a reason to these marked locations?"

Kate took the map, glanced to ensure Agatha and Vivi were well and then moved to the last chalkboard, putting up the map and making a list of the locations.

"We need to talk to Vernon and Ian as well," Violet said, knowing Rita would groan. "What do you think? Cocktails?"

"Dinner at 8:00 p.m.—someone warn Cook. Cocktails at 10:00 p.m." Rita wrote the letters quickly, spritzed perfume on them with a look of distaste, then sealed them before rising. "Now I want to play."

She crossed to the chalkboard and stared before she started writing.

**DENNY LANCASTER**—Having observed so many murder investigations, it's doubtful even someone as lazy as he would deign to put himself at risk for someone like Samuel Richards.

**LILA LANCASTER**—The only people at risk of being murdered by Lila are Martha and Denny.

**VIOLET WAKEFIELD**—She's too clever to be caught for any murder. If you find an impossible crime? Vi did it.

**JACK WAKEFIELD**—Honorable beyond belief.

**RITA RUSSELL**—A shady character, but without motive as far as Samuel Richards goes.

**HAMILTON BARNES**—Keep an eye on this one.

**VICTOR CARLYLE**—Unlikely. Where's the motive?

**KATE CARLYLE**—Maybe if it were Martha dead instead.

The constable stared at the board in confusion. "I don't understand. Is this a joke?"

"If we don't keep things light, Vi gets dark," Denny told him. "Actually, she'll get dark as soon as we slow down. Better to do what we can to figure this out and then get her to focus on doing something charitable. Vi, you should create a charity for girls."

Violet turned to Denny, who handed her Vivi. "Girls like Vivi and Agatha who aren't as lucky as these two are."

Vi frowned at Victor as he added, "You could choose likely girls and see them through their school days into some sort of training so they can care for themselves. Or what about the wives of murder victims? Or both."

"How about just woman and girls affected by murder *as well as* something for girls in general. Want to start a business? Pitch an idea to Lady Vi."

"Mmm," Vi considered. "I prefer Mrs. Wakefield."

She ignored them to take Vivi and glance through the paperwork that the constable had separated. As she sank into it, Martha rose and paced the room. Finally she crossed to Kate and demanded, "Why are you marking down the stops from the steamship? Don't you have anything better to do? Everyone acts like you're so smart and—"

"Enough," Rita said idly and Martha leapt as though Rita had shouted.

Kate scowled at the work she'd done. "It was rather obvious, I suppose."

"I suppose I should have noticed," Rita admitted, "having been on the steamship."

"That's solved, then. Kate, why don't you come help me," Violet suggested.

Kate started with the letters while Violet tried to determine the nature of the ledgers. While they worked, Rita plucked all the possible details from Martha's ridiculously vapid head.

At some point, Jane and Poppy came for the girls and Kate followed to see to their feeding. When she returned, she took up where she'd left off. Henry helped by sorting the letters according to sender and date while Denny picked up random ones to read aloud to Victor. Many of them made no sense.

After hours, Violet looked up rubbing her eyes. "If these are missionary ledgers, I'll be very surprised."

"I am almost positive," Kate said, massaging the back of her neck, "that these are coded business letters and—if I were to guess—blackmail letters." Victor crossed to her and took over kneading her neck and shoulders.

"Oh thank goodness," the constable said in relief. "I was thinking the same thing and wondering if Chief Inspector Barnes was going to see to it that I never got past constable. I would like to work for Scotland Yard someday."

Violet didn't mock him as he seemed to expect. "I think you'd be a good candidate, Constable. What's your first name?"

"Jack." Henry blushed.

"We'll call you Henry then. Jack's a common one, isn't it?"

Henry nodded.

Violet returned to the matter at hand. "Did *anyone* know him as a missionary?" She looked pointedly at Martha.

"Why would I know?"

"You were engaged to him."

"I met him on the boat so there wasn't much missionary work to do, was there?"

Vi pressed her fingers against her forehead and took in a deep breath.

"Shall we assume, then, that he wasn't a missionary? In all of his paperwork, there is not one religious document other than the Bible he carried around."

"I think that's reasonable," Kate agreed.

Violet looked at the time. "Let's see what we can find out from Rita's boys. Do we think that none of them knew about him?"

Kate shook her head as did Rita.

"In my opinion," Rita said, "looking at that pile of paperwork, whatever is going on is not a one-man job."

Violet turned to Denny and asked, "Do you have the contact information for John Smith?"

He nodded. "I love that fellow. He's about as sneaky as they come. He'd have definitely worked for Moriarty if this were a Holmes book."

"It's not," Lila reminded him. "You're obsessed."

"We should have gotten a dog before they took the good names."

"Rouge and Holmes are going to have puppies," Violet announced. "We'd let you have a little Moriarty."

"We could have the villains," Denny agreed. "We need an Adler too."

"No," Lila said. "If you're getting one of each, you need different litters or we'll have cross-eyed puppies that we'll have to bribe people to take."

"You could drown them," Martha suggested.

Violet closed her eyes before she accidentally strangled Martha. "I am napping the evening away even though it's so late. Denny, wire John Smith, rogue private investigator, and see what he can find out about Samuel Richards and Rita's men."

Denny grinned and crossed to the desk to write his own note. "I'll offer extra money to get the information before dinner with Rita's boys. That way we can go in knowing their secrets and see where we land."

"And you, Henry," Rita said, "you have a suit, right? You're going to be my cousin and my father's heir. We'll see how they bail on me."

"Ah." Henry blushed. "I don't think I have what I'd need for that."

"He could use one of Jack's suits," Victor declared, eyeing the constable. "Come with me."

"That isn't going to work," Martha snapped. "Even if fake-cousin is the heir, you're not going to be left high and dry."

"Unless we lie," Kate said. "We should lie and see what they do."

"It doesn't matter if they stay or go when they realize about the money," Rita told them. "None of them are the men for me."

"But, you have an idea, right? About who is?"

Rita didn't answer.

Victor led Henry out of the room and Violet followed to go to her own room. She needed to clear her head. And get away from Martha.

# CHAPTER 13

This murder didn't make sense. Of course, they were starting with the premise that the people who had known Richards on the ship were the most likely suspects. Violet wasn't sure she bought such a thing. Why had Samuel Richards come back to England? What had he been up to? Who had he worked with? Was whatever those ledgers showed something that had led to his death?

Of all the information they had so far, Violet would guess that Richards's most likely killer—outside of Martha—would be a partner who was committing whatever crime Richards had been up to.

Vi stared at the ledgers long after the evening should have ended. She'd tried to nap, failed, taken a bubble bath instead, and then had found her way back down the stairs to stare at the chalkboard. She leaned back on the Chesterfield and yawned deeply. There was no reason for someone like Parkington Bidlake to even pay the slightest amount of attention to Samuel Richards, let alone kill him.

Vi yawned again and then Rouge crawled into her lap. It was late into the evening, and the house had quieted down to nothing. One of the babies cried, but she was quieted before she could get a good wail going.

Vi wasn't sure when she slipped into sleep, but when she dreamed, she was holding baby Agatha and running down the pier. The sound of someone clomping after her was terrifying. Did she leap into the sea *with* the baby? Or did she try to hide the baby and then somehow get the villain to chase her? She paused too long and felt the stab into her side. Once, twice. She groaned and fell, holding Agatha close.

Vi hadn't expected dying to make her feet feel so cold. Somehow, it seemed that death should be harder. She shivered, holding the baby closer and felt the baby nuzzle her. Did Agatha know that her aunt was dying? Would she understand later how much Violet had loved her?

"Vi?"

Oh! Violet felt a tear slip out. She wasn't ready to leave Jack behind. She wanted *more* time with him. She wanted to sleep in his arms for more nights, she wanted to feel him hold her close, she wanted to see his children grow. There was so much left to do.

"Agatha, I'm sorry."

"Move, darling," Jack said and Violet frowned. His hand was on her shoulder. She gasped and the dream faded. "Come, Rouge. Move."

Vi was clutching Rouge tightly to her. "Oh, I was dreaming."

Jack pressed his finger between her brows. "I could tell, darling. You always frown so fiercely when you're having one of your dreams."

Violet let Rouge go and slowly sat up, gasping at the sharp pain in her back. She had slipped into sleep and twisted.

"That did look uncomfortable," Jack said. He lifted her, turned, and sat down with her on his lap. The night felt old and heavy, and Vi guessed he'd worked far too late. He placed his hand on the sore spot in her back and slowly dug his fingers in, working the pain away. "What did you dream?"

Violet told him, and he settled his chin on the top of her head. She told him about Victor's idea of creating a charity.

"You'd have to handle the cases yourself."

"You think I should?"

"I think you should spend as much time puzzling out how to help people as you do puzzling out who hurt someone."

Violet followed his gaze towards the chalkboards. She had turned the lamp on low when she'd come into the room, but there had been enough light from the windows to help. Now, however, it was a half-illuminated shadowland obscuring most of the boards.

"Did you discover anything?"

"I don't think he was really a missionary," Violet told Jack.

"I wondered the same thing when I looked through his bags. A few collars and quite a bit of other types of clothes? Only a Bible and not one other book or essay?"

"Who did you interview?" Violet tangled their fingers

together and laid her head against his chest. He was still rubbing the knot out in her back and Rouge was casting them both dark looks for setting her aside. Holmes had merely wagged his tail and gone back to sleep when Jack had lifted Vi.

"The steamship is gone. We spent much of the day talking to vendors and the hotel staff. There's nothing."

"If those ledgers and letters weren't so odd," Violet mused as she played with his fingers, "I'd guess it was some sort of drunken fight gone wrong. A furious stabbing, a quick shove into the water, and then regret."

"Myself as well. Or a robbery, except, Vi—he had hundreds of pounds on him. He had a decoy wallet and another that was in a special pocket in his jacket. Whoever killed him didn't take it. Not either of the wallets."

Vi frowned. That meant that either whoever killed him had no interest in his money, or they didn't realize he was carrying so much. Or—it was a crime. "What if the killer just got interrupted?"

"I don't know. The only people the hotel staff saw him interact with were Rita's suitors. Ham doesn't like that they were also who we saw him last with, but, why would any of them kill him?"

"They have to be struggling enough to be willing to try to marry a girl for her money."

"But are they?" Jack asked. "Henry said that no one came by today. If it had been you, in our early days, I'd have come by. I'd have tried to see you. I'd have had a note ready with my concerns if I was turned away. Probably with something like chocolate or flowers or both, Vi. It's not very loverly for them to have not come."

Violet hadn't thought of that. "Richards took the first chance to break things off with Martha. He dropped her the second we offered money, and he didn't try all that hard to get her back when we withdrew the offer. What if he was using her as a—as a—disguise for what he was up to?"

"That would mean that he didn't want what he was up to to be discovered."

"It's all conjecture and as possible as anything else at this point," Jack said. "What we do know is that someone killed him and dumped him under the pier. Someone left the money."

Violet stood and paced, twisting as she walked to remove the last lingering remnants of her aches. As she did, she fiddled with her wedding ring and thought. "What if he was a religious person at some point? He did have those scriptures at the edge of his tongue."

"All right—"

"I imagine that most criminal enterprises are run by... well, fellows who fought their way to their position."

"That's true."

"So let's say that young Samuel Richards scrapes together enough money to go do missionary work on one of those islands. Maybe it goes well, maybe it doesn't, but he runs out of money and he realizes, it would be so easy to—do whatever he's doing."

"Who would suspect a missionary?"

"No one," Violet said. "With the collars, the Bible, the ready phrasing, he'd slide along far more easily than some tattooed man with a pirate eyepatch, and a big gaudy rock on his little finger."

"So he started small, worked his way into something

worthy of note, and then he cut into a real criminal's profits?"

"Maybe?" Vi had no idea. It was a wildly imaginative plot she'd strung together out of nothing more than weird letters, weird ledgers, and a general dislike of the fellow. Oh, and of course, that he was dead.

"It's just as possible that he worked for some other criminal who was dissatisfied with his work."

"Or who he stole all that money from."

"Or he could have just been small-time and betrayed the wrong person and it's not some elaborate larger plan."

Violet frowned at Jack, who took her hand, spun her in a circle, and then lifted her over his shoulder. She dangled down his back. "What are you doing?"

"You'll think about it all night, Vi. Fall asleep when your mind finally shuts down, and then dream about it. We're getting hot milk, and you're going to tell me beautiful things until you sleep."

Violet grinned against his back despite the blood rushing to her head. He dropped her onto a kitchen countertop and puttered around until he had milk heating. She preferred to watch him work rather than help until he handed it to her without chocolate or sugar.

"No, no." She jumped down, adding vanilla sugar and cocoa before sipping. When they were finished, they left the dishes in the sink and retreated to their room where they took to bed and Violet told him all the beautiful things she could think of until she didn't remember the journey between a moment of describing lavender on a sunny day and the next moment when she was asleep.

She'd have been warmed to realize that Jack sat up, pulled up her covers, tucking them close around her, and watched her for long minutes to ensure the frown didn't appear between her eyebrows before he went to sleep as well.

# CHAPTER 14

*J*ohn Smith was one of those men that was so pretty, he made you think of heaven, angels, and fine art. Until you met his gaze, which was pure devilry. When Jack had been under suspicion of murder, Violet had hired Smith. When she'd needed someone who was willing to dive into illegalities to find evidence of Jack's innocence, she'd have paid any price and hired anyone. To Violet's surprise, it was Ham who had recommended Smith.

"I'm not one to be judgmental," Smith said, "but what have you all fallen into? I thought my next call from you would be because you fell in with a pack of drunken idiots who accidentally sent a museum on fire." He eyed Constable Henry, sitting near the parlor entrance in his uniform and watching Smith warily.

"That does sound like us," Denny said, "and an excellent idea, but what have you learned?"

"There isn't a missionary named Samuel Richards on

that ship or connected to the church he named. They didn't have any missionaries in those islands for years." Smith paused significantly.

"But they did at one time?" Vi asked.

"Vi," Denny started, holding up a pausing hand to Smith, "let's discuss. Scavenger hunt by candlelight, do you think we can rent a museum? Something big? Victor can create a special cocktail—"

Smith ignored Denny and continued, "Sterling Roberts."

"No!" Vi said, echoed by the gasps of her friends. "Was there a picture? A drawing? A—"

"Mother?" Smith nodded. "She sent her boy off during the height of the war when he was to be joining the army. His father told him never to come back. She said her son didn't have the heart to murder, even in the name of war. And yes, there was a picture, and yes, I stole it. We should probably return it."

Violet looked down at the framed picture in Smith's hands and gasped at the young Brother Samuel.

"Oh, I couldn't imagine," Kate said. "What does she think happened to her son?"

"Nothing," Smith said. "She thinks he's still doing the good work, but she doesn't mention his name in front of his father. He writes to her. She showed me the letters." Again there was something in his voice.

Vi waited.

"He's been all over those islands."

Violet's mouth twisted and she rubbed her temple. "Did you tell her he's dead?"

The scoffing glance from Smith was enough for Vi to know he had done no such thing. Vi didn't blame him.

Living for years for letters from a son who could never come home while his father lived and now would never come home? They weren't paying him enough to break that news.

Violet took in a deep breath, let it out slowly, and then asked, "What about the rest of them?"

"Parkington Bidlake is actually Poncy Bidlake. He's not a lord."

"Obviously," Victor, Violet, Denny, and Lila said in unison.

Smith scowled. "He's related to some baron or other. Distantly."

"What about the rest of them?"

"I couldn't find anything about Vernon Atkinson Watts. It's a miracle I found anything at all on these fellows with this short amount of time. Oscar Watts, however, is a Cambridge graduate who works for a bank."

"A bank?" Rita asked, frowning.

Uh-oh, Violet thought. There went the idea that Oscar didn't have any idea of who Rita was before the rumors of her inheritance were flying. Her father the bank magnate?

"The only one that matters," Violet started and then snapped her mouth shut. "I wonder if the one you can't find anything about is more interesting than the ones you can find something about."

Smith shrugged and then said, "Your man of business is on his way to read your ledgers. I spoke to him and suggested he come over. He said he'd be here before luncheon."

Vi nodded. Smith hadn't been able to learn much

more, but he did volunteer to discover what he could. Before he left he said, "I'll tell you this. I know a fair number of criminals. Even small operations need a few people working. Chances are—your victim's partner is the killer or knows who might be."

"You want to follow them? See what you can find?"

"I can't follow four of your suspects, and they just might be idiots who think your friend will fall for them."

Violet looked at Rita, who was frowning.

"I'm sure they were charming," Kate told Rita consolingly.

"Your heart was badly bruised," Lila added. "The attention had to be nice."

Rita groaned. "Follow Bidlake. We know he's a liar."

Violet didn't bother to point out they were all liars. She felt certain, however, that Rita knew Violet was holding back, which made it all the more compelling. Right? Vi took a long breath in and then another slower one. They needed to talk to Rita's lovers.

Smith left to find Bidlake while Kate and Violet returned to the paperwork. After several minutes, Kate asked, "What is this?"

Violet glanced at the receipt in her hand and shook her head.

"Where's it for?" Denny asked. He sounded almost as bored as Violet was as she re-read the ledgers. She had no idea what they referred to and reading the codes again that Richards used wasn't helping.

"A Markum Shipping."

"Markum Shipping?" Rita asked, looking up from her log of events. "I know that place. They helped with what

I bought while I was traveling. They're moving it from the ship to London for me."

"Oh I'm so dim," Violet said. "I didn't even look at the date. That's from this last voyage, isn't it?"

Kate nodded and suggested gently, "We should tell Jack and Ham."

Violet agreed and turned towards Henry, who looked relieved that Smith had left. He tensed again, though, when he caught Violet studying him.

"Detective Inspector Wakefield ordered me very precisely to remain here," he told her before she could ask.

"We won't leave," Violet lied. They'd leave in a moment with a compelling reason, but the sweet Henry didn't need to know that.

"The Detective Inspector warned me not to believe you."

Denny's hoot of laughter drowned at Violet's groan.

"Fine. Victor, you go."

"Why me?"

"Denny will likely be distracted by biscuits or cake or something of the like."

Denny shook his head. "Possibly a chocolate shop or an ice cream stand. I have standards. A plain butter biscuit isn't going to do much for me."

Vi handed Victor the receipt and said in a stage whisper, "Trust no one."

He tucked the receipt into his pocket with a glance to Henry and said, "Don't trust her."

Vi gasped.

"She drips lies from her mouth as easy as commonplaces. None of them are to be trusted," Victor added, gesturing at them all. "They are minions for her schemes."

Kate rose, patted Victor's cheek, and then whispered, "She'll just get vengeance later. You might be her equal normally, Victor darling, but you're not recovered from months of no sleep."

He grinned. "Do you remember last night? I don't."

"I slept the whole night," she told him with what seemed like an actual grin. "I feel like I could do anything at all."

Victor winked, kissed her on the forehead, and then grinned back at Violet. "You realize, of course, that Jack doesn't trust you not to snow this poor fellow. He warned Henry in advance."

"I realize," Violet said, "a lot of things. Mostly that I'm an idiot and Jack needs to know about that shipment before it gets sent off."

Violet lifted a commanding brow and Victor rolled his eyes and kissed her forehead as well. He said,"I suppose Jack thinks the killer might strike again."

They all looked at Henry. "Someone broke into the police station last night and riffled through Mr. Richard's things," he told them. "The Chief Inspector is concerned whoever did that might realize where the rest of Mr. Richard's things could be."

"It's a good thing, then," Denny mused lazily as he propped his feet up and crossed them, "that Jack and Ham have given up on keeping us out of the cases."

"We have worn them down, haven't we?" Vi laughed.

"You should be thanking her, Rita," Denny announced too loudly. "Once you torture Ham, forgive him, and then marry him—you'll be able to alleviate your boredom with dabbling in Ham's cases."

"I've never needed to meddle in anyone else's life to alleviate boredom."

Denny grinned when Rita didn't immediately object to the idea she'd end up with Ham.

"Leave her be, my lad," Lila ordered. She sighed into her book as Victor left to find Jack and Ham.

"I've sent for my mother," Lila announced.

"What?" Denny gasped.

"Martha will only be controlled by Rita for so long. Do we even know where she is now? Mother needs to step in, and I told her I've been feeling sick because of the baby and tired."

Denny sat up looking concerned and then crossed to her, turning her face up to his. After he examined her, he said, "You lied."

"Of course I did. I suppose I must love Martha under all the irritation, but it's hard to tell."

Speaking of being bored, Violet thought, glancing at Rita. She scratched out an idea on a scrap of paper. The people most likely to catch their overt lies were not in the house and those who could wouldn't tell. Henry was...he was...he was nothing less than a dare.

"Rita, have a look at this," Violet said, slipping a letter, and the scrap of paper, to her friend. Rita read Violet's note, glanced towards Henry and then nodded.

"It makes as much sense as the rest of this."

Violet hid her grin.

After several minutes of dull examination of papers and ledgers they'd already examined, Rita rose, stretched, and then said, "Excuse me."

Vi admired how Rita just stepped out without explanation. A few minutes later, Vi frowned. "I'm not getting any further than yesterday. She looked around the room as she stood from the table. "Have you seen my book?"

Denny shook his head and snuffled. Lila studied Violet for a moment, glanced at Henry, and said, "I believe you left it on the table in the hallway upstairs."

"Did I?" Violet strolled out of the parlor with a wink at Lila, and then shut the parlor door.

# CHAPTER 15

*V*iolet met Rita in the upstairs of the house. She'd already put on her hat and had Violet's in hand. Vi placed the cloche on her head. Her pleated navy dress with loose sleeves matched the cloche perfectly. The two of them snuck down the back stairs to the garden where there was an exit out the side of the garden for the servants. With a swift, silent glance, they followed the walk to the backstreet that wasn't overlooked by the front of the house they'd taken.

"Smith is following *Poncy*," Rita said. "Jack and Ham will be visiting the shipping place. We *could* go there and supposedly check on my things, but we'd be discovered and why would I?"

"Your luggage is just an excuse to meddle at the shipping place, but Brother Samuel was seen last with Oscar and Poncy. Oh that name is awful, it's no wonder he changed it. We need to hunt up Oscar without being discovered by Jack and Ham."

They walked towards The Cliff House Hotel with an eager eye for the men from the steamship. Felixstowe wasn't that big, so it was possible that they'd discover one of them. Violet grinned at Rita and hooked their elbows together, stepping into the shadow of a dress shop as she pointed to a passing constable.

"Do you imagine they're after us?" Rita asked. Her tone was so full of sarcasm, Vi had to just prevent herself from smacking the back of Rita's head.

"Do you imagine that if Ham and Jack thought we were really up to something they wouldn't use all their resources to keep us safe?"

"I—" Rita shook her head.

Violet lifted a brow and then admitted, "I don't believe that Jack has sent the constables out to track us, but if you look ahead of the constable, you'll notice Oscar Watts."

Rita's head turned and she gasped. "They're not even bothering to hide that they're having him followed. Look, he just nodded to the constable before looking into that window. Do you think he's wandering just to tease the man?"

"Oscar does look mischievous. Don't you think Jack and Ham decided to put pressure on those from the steamship as the most likely killers?"

"That feels ham-handed," Rita declared, winking at the term.

"Oh, I think we can do better, Rita." Vi grinned as she waved a little boy over to her and flashed several coins at him. His gazed widened and Violet said, "I'll give this to you if you go beg that constable to help you find your mama."

"My mama is buying bread," the boy said.

"Cry," Rita added, "loudly."

"That's lying."

"It's just acting," Vi suggested, feeling as though his mother might not agree or appreciate the interference. She handed him the coins. The boy stared down at the small pile.

"She's gonna be so mad," the boy said.

"But you'll have so much money for candy," Rita reminded him.

With a grin that he quickly hid with a woeful expression, he went towards the constable.

"You ready?" Rita asked.

Vi nodded, and the moment the constable was distracted by the loud wail of the boy whose performance could rival Martha's, they darted up, hooking arms with Oscar and tugging him with them into the first likely shop.

"What's all this?" Oscar asked. "Rita? Violet? What in the world?"

Rita turned and winked. "We saw you were in a predicament. Just think of us as rescuing angels. Filled with mercy, kindness, and beauty."

"Well, I think that might be Mr. Wakefield who caused my situation, no offense to you, Mrs. Wakefield."

"Vi, please," Vi grinned as she continued, lying, "Jack doesn't seem to think being friends with you a compelling reason to trust Rita and me when we say you weren't even friends with Brother Samuel."

Oscar adjusted his spectacles. "That's true enough. Didn't care for the fellow myself." A thought seemed to strike him, and he added, "Not that I'd murder him either way."

"Of course not," Rita flattered, letting him place her hand on his elbow and then covering her hand with his own. His eyes gleamed down at her with a sort of surprised happiness when she didn't pull away.

"Hello there," the proprietor of the shop said, and they turned to see they'd entered a tobacco shop. The proprietor's expression demanded that they buy something or leave.

Vi went to inquire about things for Jack and Victor while Rita continued to flirt with the surprised Oscar.

As Vi ordered somewhat randomly, Vi watched the constable go running by. "Perhaps we might make a hasty retreat towards that pub before the constable turns around?"

"Why did you help me, Vi?" Oscar asked. "I intended for the constable to have a rather boring day watching me visit the bookshop, send Rita roses, and generally wander Felixstowe. I don't have to be back to work for a few more days, and I haven't quite given up hope that—"

He glanced down at Rita and blushed.

Rita surprised him more by saying, "I hoped that you —" She blushed too, and Vi held back her question of what Rita was thinking to bring on a blush like that one.

Newly-purchased tobacco in hand, the three hurried between the tobacco shop and the pub. Oscar arranged a corner table, and they ordered pints, fish, and chips.

Vi sipped her ginger beer to Oscar's amusement. It wouldn't do to have him amused. "My grandmother loved ginger," she said, making up both her grandmother and a love of ginger. "I suppose it's a bit of a comfort thing now. I always—" She shuddered, staring into the light and letting her eyes strain against the glare until they started to tear. "I need it when I'm sad."

It worked. "Is it the murder that's making you sad? You didn't seem to be a—ah—much of a fan of the missionary."

Vi sniffed again, wiping away a tear and saw Oscar hide a scoffing look. "Being murdered by the sea? On holiday? It's just so sad. Why would anyone kill a missionary? I wasn't a particular fan of Brother Samuel, but that doesn't really make it understandable."

Oscar shook his head, but he patted Rita's hand. His thumb lingered a little too long, slowly moving over the back of her hand and wrist. "You know it was Brother Richards who pointed you out to me, Rita," he said, dismissing Violet. "He told me he'd met you with Miss Lancaster and suggested I might be very daring and introduce myself. You wouldn't have thought him to be a romantic, would you?"

Violet didn't laugh at the idea that Richards was any sort of a romantic, which she felt was one of those things that proclaimed her quite the actress. She really should win an award for not smacking his hand away and telling him money-grubbing bastards weren't going to end up with Rita. Whoever she did love—darn it—was going to be a man who, despite her wealth, loved her for herself alone.

"How did you meet Brother Samuel?" Rita asked, shooting Vi a dark look.

"Working, actually. I had taken this new position to allow me to stay in the islands, and I was traveling for my most recent position when I came across Samuel. I didn't care for him, really, so we rarely spoke."

"Didn't you?" Vi asked dryly. "Yet you spent time with him?"

There was an utter ring of truth to his statement about Brother Samuel but then Oscar shrugged and added, "When there are only so many Englishmen in a place, it's just natural to stick together. I couldn't help but know him and associate with him. Sometimes you just need to talk to someone who understands fish and chips —" He gestured to his plate and added, "Or a good cricket game."

Rita sipped from her pint, and Violet knew she was covering her need to learn more. She'd ordered a dark beer and she sighed as she set it down.

"Did you know his parishioners?" she asked. "Will his missionary work fall to pieces now? Does someone step in and shepherd those sheep instead?"

"Oh, I think so," Oscar said. "I didn't know them. Just heard stories."

Violet bit into her fish and chips to hide her own urge to demand answers. There was just something about chips. She really thought she could survive on ginger wine, chips, and the occasional roast chicken. Violet bit into the crispy potato and then glanced at Rita.

"Why did he come to Felixstowe? Was he from here?" Rita asked as she played with her own basket of fish and chips.

"I don't think so," Oscar said. "You know, your husband should really look at Bidlake. If that man is a lord, I'm St. Nicholas."

"But didn't we see you with Bidlake and Brother

Samuel before he died?" Violet asked. "We were in the bar at The Cliff House, you know? I swear I saw you."

"Didn't your husband tell you?"

"Oh he doesn't tell me things," Violet said merrily. "Jack won't turn murder into a good gossip, and he does know me so well—I do love a good gossip, don't you?"

Oscar grinned and adjusted his spectacles. "I left Bidlake and Richards. To be honest," he said to Rita, "I was quite distracted by seeing you dance with that other detective. The older, fatter one."

Violet sipped her ginger beer to keep from pointing out Oscar's clear knowledge of Rita's famous father banker, her wealth, and his desire not for Rita, but for her money. He hadn't checked on her, but he'd intended on sending her flowers? Please, Vi thought, it's a day late.

If it had been Vi and Jack or Ham and Rita, there was no question that things would have gone very differently.

"Tell me," Violet said to Oscar, grinning charmingly and ignoring how he'd sidestepped that last conversation between himself and the dead man, "what is it that you do for your company?"

"Mostly I reach out and try to develop relationships. There's a fair amount of travel in it. I'm not sure I could explain without diagrams and whatnot."

Violet "ahhhed" instead of scoffing. "I bet you miss English food when you're traveling."

"Oh, I do," Oscar agreed. "I have been gone from England for such a long time. I confess this is my fourth time having fish and chips since we've come home. I'll miss it when I'm gone again, but don't you love eating food from other countries?" The question was directed at Rita and intended to bond them and leave Vi out.

Rita allowed him to play his little game. "I do love a good curry. They don't make them the same here even when you're at a restaurant owned by someone from India."

"Or perhaps a goulash?"

"Oh yes, it's been quite a while since I've been back to Prague, but I do love getting it there."

Violet watched as they tossed the names of dishes back and forth and came to the conclusion that Oscar Watts had never once, in his life, had a truly spicy curry. She wasn't all that convinced that he'd been to Budapest. It was easy enough to look at the spoiled Vi and think she hadn't been to those places, but though she'd never been to Siam as Rita had or to Africa for a safari, Vi was hardly a London and Paris only girl. It just so happened she had eaten goulash in Prague, walked Charles Bridge, and sketched the statues there.

Vi felt like she could have picked out the dishes Oscar named from travel books more than anything else. Was he just throwing ideas out? She hadn't missed how he'd referred to his new "position" instead of his work for a bank.

Vi waited until Oscar and Rita were laughing together before she asked, "Who do you think killed Brother Samuel?"

Oscar shrugged. "I have no idea. Honestly, I don't care that much. I know that makes me seem cold, but he was hardly my dearest friend, and someone else will come along to talk cricket with me." His gaze lingered on Rita long enough to know who he hoped would take up that position.

Vi kept herself from rolling her eyes, scoffing, or

snorting, which certainly meant that she deserved one of those chocolate cocktails that Victor made.

"You know what I want to know," Rita said. "Why anyone would kill a missionary? Even one as irritating as Samuel Richards. If they'll strike down a man of God, why not us? It's a question that demands to be answered."

Oscar looked between them. "I don't think you should worry about it." There was an order in that tone. A mild one, but an order all the same. Vi shuddered. She could just see falling for Oscar's lies and then ending up under his tyrannical thumb.

"But," Rita said softly, "I don't think Brother Samuel worried about being stabbed until he was dying."

That softness had to be something Rita was *choking* on. Vi was ready to choke on it just listening to it coming from Rita.

Oscar shrugged, entirely heartlessly, and then looked beyond Rita. Violet followed his gaze and noticed the two big men she'd seen with Samuel Richards at the carnival. There was no sign of his knowing them other than the way his eyes landed on them, paused, and moved beyond.

"So you don't know anything about Brother Samuel?" Violet asked.

"I don't think you should worry about it," Oscar told them, smiling, and then reached out to take Rita's hand. "There are so many other things to garner our attentions and concerns."

Oh, Violet thought, oh no. She kept her gaze on her hand long enough to hide her disgust. "But Oscar," Rita said with a feigned fearfulness, "what if I cross someone in the street? Should I fear them all?"

"Why would you? Rita darling, whoever killed that missionary isn't going to bother you."

"Why would anyone kill a missionary and not me?" she shot back. "Surely a missionary would be even safer than I."

"He was probably murdered by someone who...who..."

Violet lifted her eyebrows and tried to look anxious about his answer.

"Well, maybe he wasn't only a missionary."

Oh ho, Vi thought sarcastically, but she gasped dramatically, fluttering her lashes and staring at Rita as though she was terrified. When Oscar looked away from Vi's dramatics, Vi shifted swiftly to a pointed look and lifted brow.

"What else was he? You know, don't you? A man of the world like yourself. Who knew him in those islands? Who else would know, but you?" Rita's eyes were wide and pleading as though his answer would deliver her from her fears.

"It's hard to live without regular work." Oscar patted Rita's hand again, never quite letting his thumb leave her wrist, stealing those unwelcome caresses. "A man such as him might make unexpected random decisions to survive that he wouldn't suspect."

Now that, Violet thought, was true. A shocking thing coming from a man she was pretty sure had been lying from the first moment he'd met Rita.

"Did you see him spend more time with one person than another?" Vi asked, trying for wide eyes and avid attention. She wasn't sure she could pull off hanging on his every word. "That's who we'll watch out for, Rita."

"Just stay home until this case is wrapped up. Supposedly, Scotland Yard is one of the most effective police forces in the world. Let them do their work."

# CHAPTER 16

"*L*et them do their work!" Violet growled to Rita as Vi stormed down the sidewalk. "Did you hear that snide tone?"

"I did," Rita said calmly. She was checking her marcelled blonde waves in her compact.

Violet groaned. "He thinks he has you in the bag. He went straight from charming to smarmy without nary a second glance."

"He did."

Rita's calm voice was making Violet nearly as furious as that condescending man.

"He did," she snapped sarcastically. "Did you notice how referred to the 'company' he worked for? He's not entirely stupid given your father is something of a famous banker. Your Oscar deliberately avoided the word 'banker.'"

"I remembered he asked me my father's name. On the steamship." Rita's calm broke with disgust. "He knew the second I told him Father's name, with the rumors of my heiresshood, he knew exactly who I was! The fiend!"

"He knew who you were from the beginning." Vi turned to Rita and hissed, "He knew who you were *and* he said that Samuel Richards told him to look to you. His lies changed, you know. At first he didn't know Richards. Then he knew him to speak to. Englishmen sticking together. Then he's getting advice from the man? Then it was that he was involved in something off? I doubt he'd know that if he didn't also know *exactly* what it was, or maybe was even a partner."

"Yes," Rita said. "Oh! I'm going to the shipping place."

Vi paused and glanced towards Rita. "Isn't it at a warehouse?"

"So? I'm their customer, aren't I? Maybe I'll hire them to get me a custom piece of something out of Siam. A wardrobe? A low table? I don't know. Something. Anything. Did you see how quickly he just assumed I'd jump into his arms? The cheek!"

Violet nodded and hurried after Rita, whose ability to rush ahead outpaced Vi's. Really, Vi thought, she needed to do more than swim and take the dogs for walks. Perhaps she could find another jiu jitsu teacher who would come with her to the country house. Spoiled beyond measure, she thought, but she was still determined to look for someone who would teach her.

Rita reached the warehouse offices, and as they rounded the side of the building, Smith stepped out from behind an auto, grabbed Rita's arm, and then jerked his head at Vi who had just caught up. They stepped into the shadows and he demanded, "What are you doing here?"

"Meddling," Vi said calmly. "I thought you were following Bidlake."

"I am. Do Wakefield and Barnes know what you two are up to?"

"We don't need keepers!"

Smith's laugh had Violet scowling and Rita smacking his arm.

"Don't forget who you work for, my lad."

"Wakefield and Barnes."

Vi lifted her brow and Smith shifted, trying for one of his pretty smiles, dimples and all.

"Mrs. Wakefield, of course," he tried.

"They're too straight for you," Rita reminded him. "Without Vi's meddling ways, you'd be left to confirming that a husband is, in fact, being cuckolded and that employees are, in fact, stealing from their employers."

"True enough," Smith agreed. "Plus Mrs. Wakefield pays better and asks more interesting questions."

"So you followed Bidlake here?" Vi demanded, bored of Smith's employment concerns.

"I did indeed. What's interesting is that he broke in through the back—"

"Let's do the same," Vi told Smith. "Rita, go cause a ruckus and get us some time."

Rita scowled but relented under Vi's look. "I suppose I am the one who hired them."

"You are indeed."

"It would be off for you to throw the ruckus."

"Mmm," Vi agreed.

"You didn't let me finish, ladies," Smith interrupted. "What's interesting is that he broke in through the back and someone else went running out."

"What did he look like?" Rita demanded.

"Gent, hat pulled low. That's all I know. I had to choose between following him and seeing what Bidlake was up to."

"Oscar Watts was with us," Rita said, considering. "Perhaps it was Vernon or Ian. I wonder if Ham had them all followed."

"I'd guess so," Vi said. "So who slipped his leash?"

Rita shrugged and stomped towards the shipping offices.

"I wonder what she's going to say," Vi mused, and then followed Smith through a locked door that he opened in a breath with the twist of his wrist and the slipping away of a tool that was out, used, and gone before she could even see it. "What would you charge to teach me that?"

"Lady Vi," Smith answered, "I prefer to continue living, and I'm just not sure your husband would allow me to do so if I were to help you be more of a meddlesome danger to humanity."

"So you won't teach me?"

"So, it'll cost you more."

Vi grinned at Smith's back and then sidled along the side of the shadowed warehouse with him. Crates were put in surprisingly straight rows with precision on each label. "I say," Vi whispered, "I'd hire these blokes. Look at this place."

"Lady Vi," Smith murmured, "with all due respect"— his tone made it clear he intended very little respect —"shut your mouth and keep it closed."

Vi shrugged and nodded, following him as quietly as

possible. His grey suit with pinstripes allowed him to slide easily between shadows. Vi, on the other hand, in her white and blue navy dress, t-strap shoes with heels, and navy cloche was likely easily observable despite the shadows.

Vi noticed how silently Smith moved and added that to her list of things to pay him to teach her. She stepped into a deeper shadow and determined to sidle into the deeper darkness behind one of the large crates when a large hand wrapped around her mouth and pulled her against his body. She'd have screamed if she didn't recognize it was Jack immediately.

Smith, however, turned in alarm. He must have only seen the hand on her mouth and her disappearance, and to Vi's delight Smith rushed after.

"It's Wakefield," Ham said low and a moment later, Smith seemed to melt into nothing. "Vernon escaped the fellow following him. When we realized, we decided to come here and see if he appeared. Vernon, however, was spooked by Bidlake."

Jack pulled Vi more firmly against his body and started back towards the exit. Vi caught a glimpse of Smith's grin and a low chuckle from Ham. In spite, she whispered, "Rita's in the office distracting them."

Jack was the one who laughed then, though it was a low, huffed thing. They slipped out through the rear door and Jack kept her hidden in the shadows with him. "I don't know why I'm surprised."

"Frankly," Vi told him, shifting around so she could cup his chin. "Henry felt a bit like a dare."

Jack's only reaction was the slight tightening of his jaw. "And what did you do with all this freedom?"

"Led Oscar on. I believe Rita will be receiving a proposal and a ring at any moment."

Jack relaxed, probably thinking she'd at least had a constable's eyes on her, keeping her safe. Vi hated to disabuse him, but it had to be done.

"There's a constable out there who is not looking forward to speaking with you."

There was that tell-tale clenching of his jaw. Vi tucked her arm around his elbow.

"You'd be so sad if I were boring like Martha."

That didn't amuse him either.

Vi grinned which seemed to further set him on edge. "Vi—"

She winked.

"My goodness woman, you're gonna drive me to my grave. Why did you insist on meddling?"

"For fun," Vi admitted then shook her head. That wasn't true at all. "It was curiosity that drove me. Rita, I think, was just angry and hurt. I couldn't let her go alone, though—we didn't really discuss it."

Jack shook his head and then sighed as he pulled her close. "Vi, we have no idea what is happening here. That puts us all at risk. I can handle just about anything, I think, as long as I have you."

Vi pressed her face into his chest. "The greyness stays away when I'm proactive, Jack. I can't just be a flower who stays home and grows in my conservatory, coddled and spoiled. That isn't who I am."

Jack pressed a kiss to the top of her head, and then tilted her face to his and kissed her breathless and stupid. They waited for Ham to come out but found Rita coming around the side of the building instead.

"Ham yelled at me."

Vi snapped her mouth shut.

"I believe that *Poncy* is at the top of the suspect list," Rita snarled. "Ham completely set aside what I tried to tell him about Oscar Watts."

"What about Oscar Watts?" Jack asked.

"He seemed to know that Brother Samuel was up to something." Vi tucked her hair behind her ear when Jack's eyes flashed with irritation.

"Where were you when you found this out?"

"Together," Rita snapped.

That wasn't the comfort Jack wanted.

"In a pub and in a tobacco shop."

"Is Jack your keeper? Are we prisoners now? Children?" Rita sneered, and Violet's head tilted as she shot daggers with her eyes at Rita. "Oh!"

Rita turned and stormed away, and Vi placed her head back against Jack's chest. "I am afraid Ham made a misstep."

"Do you know what I did when you got hurt?"

Vi shook her head.

"Lost years of my life, Vi. Ham is starting to realize that loving an independent woman is terrifying. There's a reason I bought you a gun and taught you how to shoot."

Violet didn't point out that she wasn't carrying it, but Jack knew.

"I've learned with you, Vi. I've learned to trust you and trust fate. Trust your wits, your strength, and your ability to look after yourself. Ham already feels like he's losing Rita. Better to lose her and have her be alive than to lose her from existence."

Violet nodded, understanding. She'd do just about anything to keep Jack alive. If she truly thought he were in danger? She'd tackle him, give him a guard like Henry. She'd break all the rules and probably do whatever was necessary to keep him safe, regardless of his feelings on the subject. She pressed up on her toes to kiss his face, and said, "I'm not going to stay home with a guard while you are off risking yourself."

His gaze narrowed on hers and Vi pressed another kiss on his chin before she added, "If I am doing anything with a murder again, I will at least think about bringing a gun or Denny to hide behind."

Jack didn't appreciate her joke, but he said, "I need to find out what Bidlake intended, we need to discover what Vernon Atkinson intended, and I will ensure we follow up with Oscar."

"He's coming to dinner," Vi told Jack, winking at the look on his face and then hurried after Rita.

# CHAPTER 17

*V*iolet hurried towards the house they'd taken. She felt as though she were being chased by that sick and worried look on Jack's face, and she wanted nothing more than to catch Rita up and make her understand that Ham's worry was coming out of love. As she moved towards the house, her gaze was caught by those huge men again.

They were *so* big, it seemed they could be giants in a carnival sideshow. She'd guess that they'd even tower over Jack. They were walking towards The Cliff House, and Vi frowned. She wasn't a person without friends across income lines, but there was something about men who looked like carnies making their way into a hotel that screamed an excessive amount of money.

Vi considered and then followed. She watched them go inside through the staff entrance. She followed more slowly and saw them heading down a hall and then up a set of staff lifts.

Vi got look after look as she followed. The staff would probably be referring their superiors to the odd bright young thing wandering the non-guest areas of the hotel before long. Vi ignored their looks and walked slowly but confidently after the giants. They took the staff lift to the third floor, and Violet decided to walk past the lift and find her way to the front desk.

She wanted, desperately, to follow the men, but she remembered that agonized look on Jack's face from not even a half-hour ago. She would not purposefully ignore her instincts. Instead she crossed to the manager's desk and said, "Hello."

The concierge examined her with a snotty expression.

Violet dropped the cheeriness on her face, glanced down, noted the dust and cobwebs from the warehouse, the certainly smudged lipstick from Jack, and the general shabbiness of her appearance.

"I have never been so appalled in my life!" Vi squawked. "To think that my father recommended this… this…this…flea trap."

"Lady Vi?" Oscar Watts asked, crossing to her. "Whatever happened to you?"

"These fools!" Violet snarled. "I was going to—well, never mind. You can be assured that the Carlyle family will never, EVER, recommend this hotel. In fact," Violet warned, "in fact—I will do what I can to ensure this business is destroyed."

She spun, shaking her dress off at Oscar. "Oh! Mr. Watts. I—do you have a room here?"

"Overlooking the cliff, with a view of the sea. It's quite nice, I assure you. What happened?"

Vi scoffed, glanced around, and sneered, having to channel her stepmother to truly let the disdain appear. "Top floor?"

Oscar shook his head, "Third floor, I'm afraid. Bidlake insisted on the last top floor. Used his *title.*"

Violet's sneer increased, and then she said, "Good day, Mr. Watts. I'll see you at dinner when I scrub this...this... idiocy off of me."

"Ma'am!" the concierge said, chasing after her as she left. He tried to apologize, but Violet held up a hand and demanded, "Begone with you!"

Violet stormed out the hotel with the concierge chasing after her. Violet waved him off and then paused as Jack and Ham were walking up the steps. Violet was almost certain that Jack had broken into internal curses. Ham, on the other hand, demanded, "Where is Rita?"

"She stormed off on me," Violet said. "You're going to need to beg."

Violet bypassed Jack and started towards the house they'd taken, but he called something to Ham and followed after. They walked in silence for a long stretch before Jack asked, "I assume you weren't searching rooms?"

"I saw those huge men that Brother Samuel was talking to come into the pub where Rita and I had lunch with Oscar. He noticed them but didn't give any sign of knowing them. But I saw them walking towards The Cliff House and decided to follow at a distance."

Violet had to give Jack credit—he didn't groan or shout. He just waited as he walked with her.

"Third floor," she told him. "I thought doing more

than seeing what floor the lift stopped on would be unwise."

There was a long, fraught silence until Jack said, "I'm sure you're right about that. Ian Fyfe was in the jail cells on the night of the murder, sleeping off a rather prodigious overindulgence. Oscar Watts and Parkington Bidlake both say they left the other with Brother Samuel and went inside."

"What did they say when you confronted them about their lie?"

"We haven't yet," Jack said. "Vernon doesn't have an alibi, but he also is so quiet and average-looking, not one member of the staff remembers him coming or going, at all. Both Vernon and Oscar are on the third floor, as is Ian Fyfe. Bidlake is on the fourth floor."

"What did he say about breaking into Richard's crate?" Vi asked. "He said that Richards was shipping something for him, and it occurred to Bidlake that a gentleman's agreement would not get his rather valuable item back."

"What was in the crate?"

"Small glass bottles, identified as salt."

"What was it really?"

"Cocaine," Jack said. He rubbed his jaw. "The thing is —Bidlake does seem to be the last fellow with Richards, only he was upset when he saw the contents. I am almost convinced he had no idea he was looking at cocaine instead of salt."

"What does Ham think?"

Jack frowned and admitted, "I'm not sure Ham is himself at the moment."

Violet paused at the end of the lane where their house was situated. "He needs to clear his mind and focus."

"Now that it's cocaine, Vi, the killer could be anyone. It goes from being a missionary who was murdered over a disagreement to something far more insidious and difficult to track. The local fellows had no idea that cocaine was coming through here. They're shocked, dismayed, and a little disbelieving."

Violet shook her head. "Jack, darling, you aren't thinking either. We went to a traveling carnival the night that Richards died."

Jack stared at Violet and then muttered a curse. "Where he was meeting with a couple of carnies."

Violet patted his cheek. "The carnies would have taken Richards's money and been noted. The ledgers are complex. Someone else is involved with this."

"Likely Vernon," Jack said rubbing the back of his neck. "An invisible man like that? What better way to distribute your illegalities than with people who haven't left the country, a man that no one notices like Vernon, and a man that no one would suspect?"

Violet and Jack started towards the house.

"I need to talk to Ham," Jack told her. "Are you going home this time?"

"Of course," Vi agreed. "I wasn't foolish before."

"I could wish you were less witty and brave," Jack told her, cupping her cheeks. He pressed a kiss on her forehead and then each eyebrow. "You wouldn't be you, but I would worry less."

Violet pushed up on her toes and kissed him. "I could wish the same of you, you know. But then I would never have fallen in love with you. Instead, we both need to promise to be careful."

"I can do that."

"You were in my thoughts when I decided *not* to investigate further."

"I love you, Mrs. Wakefield."

It wasn't her lack of interference that made him say it. He wouldn't have been surprised if she'd followed those men up and tried to see which room they'd entered. It was that she chose him *first* when she'd decided to be careful.

"I love you, Mr. Wakefield," she replied merrily. "I had better get inside before the neighbors call Ham and tell him there's a couple being indecent outside."

Violet stepped away, looked back and found him watching her, and winked at him. She hurried inside, bypassing everyone in the parlor to find Rita upstairs.

"You're a mouthy, opinionated, loud woman."

Rita stared at Violet. "I know. I—"

Violet held up her hand. "I am the same. Rita, we're good. We're fine. All is well here. Eat, drink, and be merry with me, darling. But, you need to apologize to Ham."

"He yelled at me."

"You terrified him."

"Jack didn't yell at you."

"Jack has wanted to wring my neck and put himself out of his misery more than once. He's used to it. You, however, are dealing with a very raw love in Ham. He already is certain he's lost you. He's already certain he's not good enough for you. He's already certain that you will never forgive him, *and*—"

"I scared him."

Violet nodded.

"He reacted like that because he loves me."

Violet nodded.

"He doesn't get to yell at me like that."

Violet nodded at that as well.

Rita frowned, looking Vi up and down. "You look like you've taken up chimney sweeping."

Instead of answering, Violet took Rita downstairs and they stared at the chalkboards as the others stared at her. It said something of Vi's commitment to the case that she didn't bother with changing clothes first.

Vi took the chalk and started writing.

**SAMUEL RICHARDS**—dead, not a missionary, had an accomplice.

**MARTHA LANCASTER**— now that cocaine is involved and smuggling, she's no longer the suspect.

**PARKINGTON BIDLAKE**—not on the 4th floor, confused by cocaine. May just be a money-grubbing fool, lying about his title.

**IAN FYFE**—locked up drunk.

**OSCAR WATTS**—Did he know the carnies? Was seen with Bidlake before he died, but Jack thinks he really did leave Bidlake and Richards together. If so, where did he go? Could he be innocent? Why is he lying about being a banker? Why was he chummy with Richards on the boat?

**VERNON ATKINSON**—Did he know the carnies? Easily overlooked. *Why* was he at the shipping place if he wasn't part of the scheme?

**THOSE TWO BIG BLOKES FROM THE FAIR—**
Cocaine distributors.

Violet explained what she'd learned as she filled in the details. After long moments, Vi crossed out every name except for Oscar Watts and Vernon Atkinson.

"I don't like either of them," Denny said. "The one knew where the cocaine was but didn't get into the crate. Could he just be stealing from the dead man? We don't know anything about him. The other one? He's been lying from the beginning, he knew Richards, he knew who Rita was. He's a snake."

"But," Lila inserted lazily, "he's a snake that might only be after her money."

"Or, he's a murderous snake."

"Only one of them could have done it," Victor said. "And you've invited them to the house this evening. It occurs to me that I'll be taking the nannies, the babies, and Kate and leaving. Violet, darling, maybe you should cancel dinner?"

Vi shook her head. "Take them and go. They come before any of the rest of this."

Victor pressed a kiss to her forehead and suggested, "You should slip that derringer into your dress, Vi. Or strap it to your leg. Be careful."

"Did Fredricks come?"

"He took the ledgers and left," Victor said. "Your man of business has rather a lot to keep him busy, but he looked them ledgers over enough to agree with Smith. This scheme—whatever it is—being an operation large enough to have more than one man."

"Be careful," Violet ordered Victor. He laughed at her as he hurried up the steps after his girls. She watched him hurry them out of the house and then faced Denny.

"Did you want to send Lila away?"

"If I did," he said, "who would protect me?"

## CHAPTER 18

*V*iolet was wearing an aqua dress that reached to the floor with a long slit up her leg. It tucked closed around her chest and torso, dipping low between her breasts with a long flowing swathe of fabric from her waist to the ground. She layered her favorite diamond choker around her throat and added the long strand of turquoise beads that Victor had bought her what seemed like ages ago in Cuba.

The derringer was strapped to her thigh just above the slit, making for easy access but also leaving no reason to believe that it was there. She kohled her eyes, rouged her cheeks and lips, carefully powdered her nose, and applied layer after layer of mascara.

For a random dinner by the sea with two murder suspects, Violet admitted she was dressing carefully because she felt bad about sneaking out from Jack's protection. If he appreciated her efforts, maybe they'd only bring it up every time it was convenient for whatever argument they were having for the rest of their lives?

She smirked and then glanced up as Lila stepped into the room. Her long, tight dress reflected the smallest of bumps where her normally flat stomach curved out.

"Look at you," Vi gasped. "Look at that baby! She's my second favorite! The twins are tied, of course. You should name this one Violet the Third!"

"Pass," Lila said idly. "Though perhaps we'll call her Ruby."

"For a woman more valuable than rubies?"

"Indeed," Lila said. "It's the best of the stupid names Denny keeps begging for. Are you in a good mood?"

"Sure, we're having dinner with likely murderers, liars, and general cheats. What's not to enjoy?"

"Ah, yes. Well. Jack and Ham have taken in Bidlake on a suspicion of murder and send their regrets."

Violet's gaze narrowed. "What about Oscar and Vernon? They're far more obvious."

"Denny asked them that when Jack telephoned. He was told to keep out of it."

Violet groaned. "They think that having lied about his name and status, and having been with Richards the night of his death, broken into the supply crate, and generally being irritating is reason enough?"

"I am guessing that might be it," Lila said. "I would suggest we should cancel dinner, but it seems rude after just inviting Vernon along as well."

"What does Rita say?"

"She needs her mouth washed out with soap."

Violet leaned back and sighed. "Someone had a

servant wash the chalkboards and remove them from the parlor, right?"

"Denny said he would tell the servants to take care of it," Lila said.

Before Violet could reply, Rita came into the room. "Did you hear they arrested *Poncy?*"

Violet nodded, glancing Rita over. Her dress was fringed, sapphire, and made her look like a precious jewel. "You are unfairly beautiful."

Rita rolled her eyes. She looked Lila over. "Do I see the beginning of a baby there?"

Lila started to answer, but the doorbell rang. "Dinner."

"With murderers," Rita said darkly.

"Jack and Ham wouldn't have not come if they were worried for our safety," Vi said as she stepped out of her room.

"Henry is in the kitchens," Lila said helpfully and with an underlying sarcasm. "He's got a steak and potatoes in front of him with a look of pure glee on his face. Should something happen, I believe he's already too stuffed to be able to help."

"Nothing is going to happen," Rita reassured her. "There's too many of us and there's no hiding who did it."

Violet didn't disagree. As she passed a mirror in the hallway, she glanced at her reflection, felt beautiful, and wished Jack were there. Maybe after he finished whatever he was doing, they could go for a walk by the sea. She didn't care if her dress wasn't ideal for walking on a pebble shore. She loved it and wanted to wear it.

"We need to go to a party," Violet said, "in this dress. I love it."

~

"WE NEED DRINKS," Denny said after dinner. "I've been practicing that chocolate cocktail."

"Intriguing," Oscar said smoothly. "That does sound nice."

Oh heavens yes, Violet agreed silently. Watching Oscar rub Rita's wrist with his thumb, watching Rita simper, and attempting to pull Vernon into a conversation was enough to make Vi go mad. She was generally irritated with Jack for not being there and with Ham for the look of rising fury Rita was fighting to hide. The only positive had been the lack of Martha, who had disappeared somewhere, but no one was bothered by it. Violet rather hoped she was on a train back to her mother.

"Rita, darling," Oscar said, "perhaps once we have had our cocktails, you'd be willing to walk with me on the beach."

Violet winced for Rita, who fluttered her lashes, glanced down to hide her fury, and then looked back up with flushed cheeks. Anyone who didn't know her would assume that blush was because she knew another marriage proposal was coming. Oscar adjusted his glasses and didn't bother to hide his triumph.

"Cocktails," Violet muttered under her breath. She turned to Vernon. "Do you like chocolate?"

He shook his head. "It gives me headaches."

Violet contained her scoff. Lila grinned, not even bothering to hide her reaction. Denny saw his wife's smile, giggled, and then told Vernon, "Too sad, old man."

Denny was the one who opened the parlor door and let Oscar and Rita step through the door together followed by Violet and Vernon. Lila and Denny were next and all of them stopped, staring towards the chalk-boards that had not—in fact—been removed.

"Oh. I believe I may have forgotten something," Denny said with a high-pitched giggle. "Sorry Vi!"

Lila rolled her eyes as she crossed to a chair and took a seat. "Oh laddie."

"Denny!" Rita hissed and then faced Oscar whose gaze had narrowed but his face was relatively calm.

Still his voice was pure ice as he asked, "Is this what you think of me? You've been throwing yourself at me and you think I killed Richards?"

"Throwing herself at you," Violet hissed and Lila shook her head. "Men."

"Look at the board," Vernon snapped. "Look at it!"

"Calm down," Oscar said evenly.

Vi read the board again, frowning, but her heart was racing. Vernon was terrified. His gaze was fixed on the part where they'd written he was working *with* Oscar. The way he turned to Oscar in that moment? Vernon was clearly the underling.


OSCAR WATTS—Dɪᴅ he know the carnies? Was seen with Bidlake before he died, but Jack thinks he really did leave Bidlake and Richards together. If so, where did he go? Why is he lying about being a banker? Why was he chummy with Richards on the boat? He stayed behind with Richards. He had the best opportunity to kill the man. Killer? Probably. Working together with Vernon to set up Bidlake.

· · ·

VERNON ATKINSON—DID he know the carnies? Easily overlooked. *Why* was he at the shipping place if he wasn't part of the scheme? Looks like a killer. Bidlake said he had drinks with Atkinson, but Atkinson says otherwise. Clearly—Vernon and Oscar were working together to get rid of Richards and take over the business.

OSCAR'S BREATH was moving quickly, but other than that he hadn't shown any other reaction. Vernon, however, was panicking.

"Calm down," Oscar told Vernon. "Why are you so upset?"

"Upset?" Vernon's voice pitched several octaves higher. "How did they—"

Denny giggled and crossed to the bar. He started making a round of cocktails as though this were any other evening.

"Quiet!" Oscar said. "I'll take that cocktail now."

Denny loaded a silver tray with his drinks, delivered one to Oscar, one to Vernon, one to Rita, and left the silver tray next to Lila with two more drinks. Denny moved like a rabbit surrounded by snakes, keeping an eye on the two men. Vernon was panicking, Oscar was becoming colder and colder, and Denny was feeling the pressure of it all. Through it all, Violet was thinking of how upset Jack would be that this occurred.

"Do you think this?" Oscar asked, gesturing at the board.

"Yes," Rita said simply. "You obviously were working with Richards, his ledgers prove it. You are going to be arrested for smuggling cocaine and murdering the man you worked with to set it all up."

"They already arrested Bidlake."

"They know he didn't do it," Rita lied as she lifted a mocking brow. "Do you think detectives as well-known as Barnes and Wakefield don't know it was you? The only reason Bidlake got taken in was that the locals insisted. Why do you think they've got a man searching your rooms right now?"

Vernon squeaked and headed for the door, but Oscar snapped, "Stay here, fool."

Rita jumped and took a step away from him, but he snatched her wrist. Violet pressed a hand to her chest and turned just slightly so her leg was out of view.

"Oh Rita," Oscar said. "You were going to be so convenient. A well-established adventurous who travels the world with a huge inheritance? Could my cover have been any better?"

Rita bit down on her bottom lip, and while she didn't try to get away, Vi had little doubt Rita knew how. He was a fool if he thought that Rita wouldn't fight him every inch of the way. Oscar stepped forward and cupped her face. It was so very like when Jack did the same to Vi, but the way Oscar's fingers curled around the back of Rita's neck made Violet shiver. He spun Rita around and then scowled at Violet.

"I'd heard you were trouble, but given the way you blithely pranced around Felixstowe, I assumed it was nonsense."

Violet shrugged, using the motion to pull the derringer from her leg carefully and hide it in her hand as she wrapped an arm around her body. She crossed to

Denny and accepted the chocolate cocktail with her free hand.

"Vernon set up Bidlake while you killed Richards, obviously," Violet said. "The only question I have left was how you let the ledgers get out of your grasp when you had everything else in order."

"It was supposed to look like a robbery, and I intended to take his keys but that drunken Fyfe came along before I could finish. The drunk fool was being chased by constables, so I was forced to shove Richards in the water and hide. Can you imagine? He actually thought he was in love with Rita."

Violet looked at Rita. That did make sense as to why the money hadn't been taken; it was one of things that had been bothering Vi.

"Richards didn't have the imagination to truly make money. He still accepted his missionary donations and pursued that as aggressively as he pursued our work. It was a hodge-podge of side ventures, none of which paid out sufficiently for my needs."

"Well," Violet agreed and then started when she saw Oscar pull his own pistol from his pocket but continued as though she were unconcerned, "not if you wanted to be truly wealthy."

"It isn't just about money. It's also about power. Which I have and you don't. How does it feel to be helpless?"

Denny giggled and then gasped as the gun was pointed at him. "Here now. Why don't we put that thing away?"

Oscar's disgusted look had Denny holding up his hands, but it didn't last, and he lowered them to start on another round of cocktails as though that might appease Oscar.

"You should consider your choices," Rita told Oscar. "What are you going to do? Kill us all and run? Jack and Ham will hunt you until you're dead."

Oscar laughed coldly. "I'll be leaving England again tonight. They don't have jurisdiction elsewhere."

Denny choked on another giggle, probably thinking what Violet was—Jack would care little about law and order if he were pursuing the man who killed his family.

"Oscar, let's think this through," Vernon said desperately. "They're right. That Wakefield won't stop hunting for us. You can tell he loves his wife. His eyes follow her everywhere."

"Hunting for *me*," Oscar said evenly. "I'm sorry, Vernon, but you're going to have to go."

Vernon squeaked.

"Someone needs to be the villain who doesn't—quite —survive."

"But, but, you can't!" Vernon said, trying to circle away. Oscar shoved Rita back, throwing her towards the floor and she cried out in pain. Lila gasped, then went still. Her gaze was narrowed on Rita, pale with fury.

Violet only had one shot and a very small gun. She met Lila's gaze and they both glanced at Rita, who was holding her hand to her chest. The hand looked broken and Lila's anger had not faded.

Lila calmly removed the cocktails from the silver tray as Oscar laughed and straightened his arm towards Vernon.

"Don't," Vernon gasped. "Please."

"Funny," Oscar told him with that charming smile, "that's what Richards said."

Vernon turned to run and Oscar's face shifted from cold to deadly. But Lila had silently risen, silver cocktail tray in hand, and swung it like a champion cricket player up to bat. The gun went off, Vernon screamed shrilly, echoed by Denny, and Oscar crumpled. Violet rushed across the room as Oscar rolled onto his back. She held the derringer to his head as Lila took his gun.

"Denny darling," Lila said idly, "if you're done screaming, you could do us a favor and call for the constables."

Denny stared at his wife, a shrill, hysterical sound escaping. He pushed Vernon aside to go for the telephone.

"Don't," Lila said when Vernon tried to sidle away. Before he could make it two steps, Smith and Henry appeared in the doorway. Henry looked alarmed and breathless. Smith looked beautiful and amused.

"Oh," Henry said and then rushed into the room.

"I believe I have your man," Violet told him, sliding her derringer back into its thigh holster.

Smith laughed, crossing to take the gun from Lila. She looked down at Oscar, looked at Rita, and then helped her to her feet.

"Well," Lila told Rita, "I've been thinking it for days, but outside of Ham, you really do have the worst taste in men."

"Shut up," Rita said, flatly. Followed by, "I could really use a drink."

## CHAPTER 19

*H*am and Jack arrived with a screech of tires outside. They thundered up the steps and then stared in consternation at Rita, Lila, and Violet. The three of them were lined up on the Chesterfield, evening gowns straightened, chocolate cocktails in hand, watching as Smith and Henry bound the villains.

"He is pretty," Rita told Violet, tucking her arm next to her chest to lean forward and admire Smith's behind.

"They don't get prettier."

Smith looked over and flashed a dimple. "You three are too much trouble for me."

"Oh no," Lila told him, lifting her cocktail in salute. "We don't *want* you, Smith. But you are attractive. Like a very fine horse."

"Or a nice pair of shoes," Violet added thoughtfully. "One of those hand-crafted silver handbags that look like a lion, with citrine eyes. Gorgeous, fun, but unnecessary."

Rita, however, said nothing. Her gaze was fixed on

Ham. His was fixed on her. Unlike Jack, who had taken in that Violet was fine and moved from worried to calm, Ham was stuck on the sick, horrified terror.

"What were you thinking?" he demanded, taking in her hurt hand and muttering to a constable to send for the doctor.

"All my fault," Denny said, offering a tray of cocktails to the incoming constables. "I forgot to tell the servants to clean and remove the chalkboards. I'm afraid things went south rather fast after that."

"Only an idiot would have believed it was Bidlake," Rita told Ham dryly. "You should have been here."

His gaze narrowed on hers and his ears turned red.

Vi winced. She wasn't sure she'd seen Ham well and truly angry ever. He had a preternatural ability to keep calm. Did he feel naked now that Rita had stripped that away from him?

Ham swallowed thickly.

Like a lion taking down a gazelle, Rita stood. "You were wrong."

"You aren't a detective."

"Fine. Then I was just having dinner with friends."

"You thought he was a murderer," Ham roared, losing the last scraps of composure.

"Then I guess you should have shown up to dinner," Rita snapped back.

His eyes narrowed on her and then he reached out, snatched her good wrist, and pulled her closer. He took gentle hold of her neck and asked silkily, "Are these bruises?"

Rita rolled her eyes in answer, but Ham didn't see. He crossed to the two men and demanded, "Who?"

Vernon frantically jerked his head towards Oscar. Ham hauled the man up as though he were a wet kitten, and dragged him from the parlor. The sound of flesh hitting flesh followed.

"Romantic," Lila murmured. "I enjoy a good descent into caveman."

"If he thinks that beating someone is going to change things," Rita started, snapping her mouth shut when Ham reappeared in the doorway. He was so angry it was like the crackling of a bonfire.

"Take care of this mess, Henry."

The constable nodded swiftly, eyes to the ground.

This time, Ham hauled Rita against his chest. "You're going to drive me to an early grave."

"Am I?"

His answer was a kiss so thorough, Violet had to look away.

Jack smiled down at her. "Do you think this is it? Are they done now?"

Lila laughed sarcastically and Violet's explanation was simple. "I have yet to see begging."

## THE END

HULLO FRIENDS! Once again, it's my chance to tell you how much I appreciate you reading the Vi books and traveling on her journey with me. If you wouldn't mind, I would be so grateful for a review.

· · ·

THE SEQUEL to this book is available now.

**All Hallows, 1925**

Vi Wakefield decides it is time to embrace the fun. She's arranging a scavenger hunt with prizes, specialty cocktails, and costumes.

What she doesn't expect is a series of pranks that ends in a body. Once again, Vi, Jack, and friends are faced with a body, a series of mean and quite dangerous pranks, and the baffling cruelties of mankind. Will they be able to discover what is happening and why, or will this criminal escape into the night?

Order your copy here.

A new paranormal 1920s series is now available.

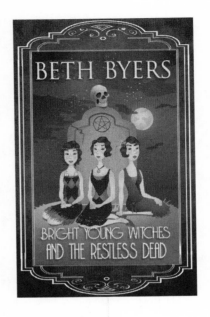

## April 1922

When the Klu Klux Klan appears at the door of the Wode sisters, they decide it's time to visit the ancestral home in England.

With squabbling between the sisters, it takes them too long to realize that their new friend is being haunted. Now they'll have to set aside their fight, discover just why their friend is being haunted, and what they're going to do about it. Will they rid their friend of the ghost and out themselves as witches? Or will they look away?

Join the Wode as they rise up and embrace just who and

what they are in this newest historical mystery adventure.

Order your copy here.

THERE IS ALSO a new 1920s series about two best friends, written by one of my best friends and I. If you'd like to check it out, keep on flipping for the first chapter.

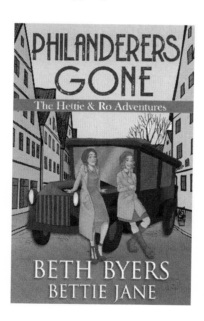

**July 1922**

If there's one thing to draw you together, it's shared misery.

Hettie and Ro married manipulative, lying, money-grubbing pigs. Therefore, they were instant friends. When those philandering dirtbags died, they found themselves the subjects of a murder investigation. Did they kill their husbands? No. Did they joke about it? Maybe. Do they need to find the killer before the crime is pinned on them? They do!

Join Hettie and Ro and their growing friendship as they delve into their own lives to find a killer, a best friend, and perhaps a brighter new outlook.

Order your copy here or keep scrolling to read more.

# PREVIEW OF PHILANDERER GONE

## CHAPTER ONE

*T*he house was one of those ancient stone artisan-crafted monstrosities that silently, if garishly, announced out and out *buckets* of bullion, ready money, the green, call it what you would, these folks were simply rolling in the good life. The windows were stained glass with roses and stars. The floor was wide-planked dark wood that was probably some Egyptian wood carried by camel and horse through deserts to the house.

Hettie hid a smirk when a very tall, beautiful, uniformed man slid through the crowd and leaned down, holding a tray of champagne and cocktails in front of her with a lascivious gaze. She wasn't quite sure if he appreciated the irony of his status as human art for the party, or if he embraced it and the opportunity it gave him to romance bored wives.

She was, very much, a bored wife. Or, maybe disillusioned was the better word. She took yet another flute of champagne and curled into the chair, pulling up her legs, leaving her shoes behind.

The sight of her husband laughing uproariously with a drink in each hand made her want to skip over to him and toss her champagne into his face. He had been drinking and partying so heavily, he'd become yellowed. The dark circles under his eyes emphasized his utter depravity. Or, then again, perhaps that was the disillusionment once again. Which came first? The depravity or the dark circles?

"Fiendish brute," Hettie muttered, lifting her glass to her own, personal animal. Her husband, Harvey, wrapped his arm around another bloke, laughing into his face so raucously the poor man must have felt as though he'd stepped into a summer rainstorm.

"Indeed," a woman said and Hettie flinched, biting back a gasp to twist in the chair and see who had overheard her.

What a shocker! If Hettie had realized that anyone was around instead of a part of that drunken sea of flesh, she'd have insulted him non-verbally. It was quite satisfying to speak her feelings out loud. Heaven knew he deserved every ounce of criticism. She had nothing against dancing, jazz, cocktails, or adventure. She did, however, have quite a lot against Harvey.

He had discovered her in Quebec City. Or rather he'd discovered she was an heiress and then pretended to *discover* her. He'd written her love letters and poems, praising her green eyes, her red hair, and her pale skin as though being nearly dead-girl white were something to be envied. He'd made her feel beautiful even though she tended towards the plump, and he'd seemed oblivious to the spots she'd been dealing with on her chin and jawline through all of those months.

A fraud in more ways than Hettie could count, he'd spent the subsequent months prostrating himself at her feet, romancing her, wearing down her defenses until she'd strapped on the old white dress and discovered she'd gotten a drunken, spoiled, rude, lying ball and chain.

"Do you hate him too?" Hettie asked, wondering if she were commiserating with one of her husband's lovers. She would hardly be surprised.

"Oh so much so," the woman said. Her gaze met Hettie's and then she snorted. "Such a wart. Makes everything a misery. It's a wonder that no one has clocked him over the back of the head yet."

Hettie shocked herself with a laugh, totally unprepared to instantly adore one of her husband's mistresses, but they seemed to share more than one thing in common. "If only!"

She lifted her glass in toast to the woman, who grinned and lifted her own back. "Cheers, darling."

"So, are you one of his lovers?" the woman asked after they had drunk.

"Wife," Hettie said and the woman's gaze widened.

"Wife? I hardly think so."

"Believe me," Hettie replied. "I wish it wasn't so."

"As his wife," the woman said with a frown, "I fear I must dispute your claim."

Hettie's gaze narrowed and she glanced back at Harvey. His blonde hair had been pomaded back, but some hijinks had caused the seal on the pomade to shift and it was flopping about in greasy lanks. He had a drink in front of him and the man he'd been molesting earlier had one as well. The two clanked their glasses together and guzzled the cocktails. Harvey leaned into the man and they both laughed raucously.

"Idiot," the woman said. "Look at him gulping down a drink that anyone with taste would have sipped. The blonde one, he must be yours?"

Hettie nodded with disgust and grimaced. "Unfortunately, yes, the blond wart with the pomade gone wrong is my unfortunate ball and chain. So the other fool is yours?"

The woman laughed. "I suppose I sounded almost jealous. I wasn't, you know. I'd have been happy if Leonard was yours."

"Alas, my fate has been saddled with yon blonde horse, Harvey."

They grinned at each other and then the other woman held out her hand. "Ro Lavender, so pleased to meet someone with my same ill-fate. Makes me feel less alone."

Hettie looked at that fiend of hers, then held out her own hand. "Hettie Hughes. I thought Leonard's last name was Ripley."

"Oh, it is," Ro said. "I try not to tie myself to his wagon unless it benefits me. At the bank, for instance."

Ro was a breath of fresh air. Hettie decided nothing else would do except to keep her close. "Shall we be bosom friends?" Hettie asked.

"I just read that book," Ro said. "Do you love it as well?"

"I'm Canadian," Hettie replied, standing to twine her arm through Ro's. "Of course I've read it. Anne, Green

Gables, Diana, Gilbert, Marilla, and Prince Edward Island were fed to me with milk as a babe. Only those of us with a fiendish brute for a husband can truly understand the agony of another. How did you get caught?"

"Family pressure. We were raised together. Quite close friends over the holidays, but I never knew the real him until after."

Hettie winced. "Love letters for me," she said disgustedly. "You'd think modern women such as ourselves wouldn't have been quite so…"

"Stupid," Ro replied, tucking her bobbed hair behind her ear.

The laughter from the crowd around the table became too much to hear anything and Hettie raised her voice to ask, "Why are we here? Shall we escape into the nighttime?"

"Let's go to Prince Edward Island," Ro joked. "Is it magical there? I've always wanted to go."

"I've never been," Hettie admitted, "but I have a sudden desperate need. Let's flee. You know they won't miss us until their fathers insist they arrive with their respectable wives on their arms."

"Or," Ro joked, "I could murder yours and you could murder mine, and we could create our freedom. If our families want respectable, I would definitely respect a woman that could rid herself of these monsters."

"That sounds lovely. Until we can plan our permanent freedom, I suppose our best option is simply to disappear into the night."

Ro lifted her glass in salute and sipped.

Hettie set aside her champagne flute, slipped on her shoes, and then turned to face her husband, who had pulled Mrs. Stone, the obvious trollop, into his lap and was kissing her extravagantly. Hettie scrunched up her nose and gagged a little. Mrs. Stone had been in Nathan Brighton's lap last week.

"She slept with Leonard too," Ro informed Hettie with an even tone.

Hettie reveled in the camaraderie she found in Ro's resigned tone. "Have you met Mr. Stone?"

Ro nodded. "He doesn't realize. He's not the type of man to be cuckolded like this. So...overtly. Have you heard of the marriage act they've proposed?"

Hettie nodded with little doubt that her eyes had brightened like that of a child at Christmas. "I will be there on the very first day. If Harvey had any idea, any at all, he'd be rolling over in his future grave. The money's mine, you know? My aunt never liked Harvey and she tied up my money tightly. He gets what he wants because it's easier to give it to him than listen to him whine, but he won't get a half-penny from me the day I can file divorce papers. They say it's going to go through."

"I couldn't care less about the money," Ro replied. "Though my money is coming from a still-living aunt. Leonard has enough, I suppose, but his eye is definitely on Aunt Bette's fortune."

"So," Hettie joked, "he needs to go before she does."

Ro choked on a laugh and cough-laughed so hard she was wiping away tears.

"Darling!" Harvey hollered across the room. "We're going down to Leonard's yacht. You can get yourself home, can't you?"

Hettie closed her eyes for a moment before answering. "Of course I can. Don't fall in." She crossed her fingers so only Ro could see. Ro's laugh made Hettie grin at Harvey. He gave her a bit of a confused look. Certainly he had shouted his exit with the hope she wouldn't scold him. Foolish man! She'd welcome him moving into Mrs. Stone's bed permanently and leaving his wife behind.

The handsome servant from earlier picked up Hettie's abandoned glass and shot her a telling, not quite disapproving look.

"Oh ho," Hettie said, making sure the man heard her. "We've been overheard."

"We've been eavesdropped," Ro agreed. Then with a lifted brow to the human art serving champagne, she said, "Boy, our husbands are aware of our lack of love. There's no chance for blackmail here."

"Does your aunt feel the same?" he asked insinuatingly.

Hettie stiffened, but Ro simply laughed. "Do you think she hasn't heard the tale of that lush Leonard? She's written me stiff upper lip letters. Watch your step and your mouth or you'll lose your position despite your pretty face. It doesn't matter how you feel, only how you look. No one is paying you to think."

The servant flushed and bowed deeply, shooting them both a furious expression before backing away silently.

"Cheeky lad," Hettie muttered. "You scolded him furiously. Are you sure you weren't letting out your rage on the poor fellow?"

"Cheeky yes," Ro agreed. She placed a finger on her lip as she considered Hettie's question and then agreed. "Too harsh as well. I suppose I would need to apologize if he didn't threaten to blackmail me."

"But pretty," they said nearly in unison, then laughed

as the servant overhead them and gave them a combined sultry glance.

"No, no, boyo," Ro told him. "Toddle off now, darling. We've had quite our fill of philandering, reckless men. You've missed your window." Ro's head cocked as she glanced Hettie over. "Shall we?"

"Shall we what, love?"

Ro grinned wickedly. "Shall we be bosom friends then? Soul sisters after one shared breath?"

"Let's," Hettie nodded. "As the man I thought was my soulmate was an utter disaster, I'll take a soul sister as a replacement."

They sent a servant to summon Hettie's driver. "I was thinking of going to a bottle party later. At a bath house? That might distract us."

Hettie cocked her head as she considered. "Harvey *does* expect me to go home."

Ro lifted her brows and waited.

"So we must, of course, disillusion him as perfectly as he has me."

"There we go! It's only fair," Ro cheered, shaking her hands over her head. "I have been considering a trip to the Paris fashion salons."

"Yes," Hettie immediately agreed, knowing it would enrage Harvey, who preferred her tucked away in case he wanted her. "We should linger in Paris or swing over to Spain."

"Oooh, Spain!"

"Italy," Hettie suggested, just to see if Ro would agree.

"Yes!"

"Russia?"

Ro paused. "Perhaps Cote d'Azur? Egypt? Somewhere

warmer. I always think of snow when I think of Russia, and I only like it with cocoa and sleigh rides. Perhaps only one or two days a year."

"Agreed—" Hettie trailed off, eyes wide, as she saw Mrs. Stone enthusiastically kiss the cheeky servant from earlier and then adjust her coat. She winked at Hettie on the way out, caring little that both of them knew Mrs. Stone would be climbing into Harvey's bed later. Or, perhaps it was Harvey who would be climbing into *Mr.* Stone's bed. "Is her husband really blind to it?"

"Oh yes," Ro laughed. "He's quite a bit older you know, and even more old-fashioned than my grandfather. He's Victorian through and through. He probably has a codicil in the will about her remarrying. The type of things that cuts her off if she doesn't remain true to him. Especially since he's in his seventies, and she's thirty? Perhaps?"

Hettie shook her head. "They have a rather outstanding blackberry wine here," she said, putting Mrs. Stone out of her mind. "Shall we—ah—borrow a bottle or two?"

Ro nodded and walked across to the bar. She dug through the bottles and pulled out a full bottle of blackberry wine, another of gin, and a third of a citrus liqueur. "Hopefully someone will think to bring good mixers." She handed one of the bottles to Hettie before tucking one under each arm.

The butler eyed them askance as they asked for their coats.

"Don't worry, luv," Ro told the butler. "Your master doesn't mind."

None of them believed that whopper of a lie, but Ro's cheerful proclamation made it seem acceptable.

"Thief," Hettie hissed innocently as her driver, Peterson, opened the door for them and they dove inside. She struggled with the cork and then asked, "Are we going nude or shall we grab bathing costumes?"

"My brother-in-law lives with us," Ro said, looking disgusted, "I'll be going nude before I go back and face that one. Look—" Her head cocked as the black cab sped up. "I think that's him! We can rush back to collect my bathing costume before he returns to the house."

"I'm a bit too round to want to go full starkers."

"The men love the curves," Ro told her. "If you wanted to step out on your Harvey, you'd need to up the attitude and cast a come hither gaze."

"Like this?" Hettie asked, attempting one but feeling as though she must look like she had something in her eye.

"Like this," Ro countered, glancing at Hettie out of the corner of her eye. "I'm thinking of a really nice plate of biscuits."

Hettie tried it and Ro bit back a laugh. "Are you angry with the biscuits?"

"Let me try imagining cakes. I do prefer a lemon cake." Hettie glanced at Ro out of the corner of her eye, imagining a heavily iced lemon cake, and then smiled just a little.

"No, no," Ro said, showing Hettie again what to do.

"Oh! I know." Hettie imagined the divorce act that Parliament was considering.

"Yes! Now you've got it! Was it a box of chocolates?"

Hettie confessed, sending Ro into a bout of laughter

and tears that saw them all the way to Hettie's hotel room. From her hotel room to Ro's house, there were random bursts of giggles and stray tears. Once they reached to bath house, Ro said, "I'll be drinking to that divorce act tonight. Possibly for the rest of my life."

"If it frees me," Hettie told Ro dryly, "I'd paper my house with a copy of it to celebrate those who saved us from a fate I should have known better than to fall into."

IF YOU ENJOYED THIS SAMPLE, you can get the full book here.

ALSO BY BETH BYERS

THE VIOLET CARLYLE COZY HISTORICAL
MYSTERIES

Murder & the Heir

Murder at Kennington House

Murder at the Folly

A Merry Little Murder

New Year's Madness: A Short Story Anthology

Valentine's Madness: A Short Story Anthology

Murder Among the Roses

Murder in the Shallows

Gin & Murder

Obsidian Murder

Murder at the Ladies Club

Weddings Vows & Murder

A Jazzy Little Murder

Murder by Chocolate

Candlelit Madness: A Short Story Anthology

A Friendly Little Murder

Murder by the Sea

Murder On All Hallows

Murder in the Shadows

A Jolly Little Murder

Christmas Madness: A Short Story Anthology

Hijinks & Murder

Lover & Murder

A Zestful Little Murder (coming soon)

A Murder Most Odd (coming soon)

Nearly A Murder (coming soon)


## THE POISON INK MYSTERIES

Death By the Book

Death Witnessed

Death by Blackmail

Death Misconstrued

Deathly Ever After

Death in the Mirror

A Merry Little Death

Death Between the Pages (coming soon)


## THE 2ND CHANCE DINER MYSTERIES

Spaghetti, Meatballs, & Murder

Cookies & Catastrophe

Poison & Pie

Double Mocha Murder

Cinnamon Rolls & Cyanide

Tea & Temptation

Donuts & Danger

Scones & Scandal

Lemonade & Loathing

Wedding Cake & Woe

Honeymoons & Honeydew

The Pumpkin Problem


THE HETTIE & RO ADEVENTURES


Candlelit Madness (prequel short story)

Philanderers Gone

Adventurer Gone

Holiday Gone

Aeronaut Gone

Made in the USA
Coppell, TX
16 February 2020